The SMIDGENS

Books by David O'Connell

The Chocolate Factory Ghost
The Dentist of Darkness
The Revenge of the Invisible Giant

The Smidgens

The SMiDGENS

DAVID O'CONNELL

Illustrated by
SEB
BURNETT

BLOOMSBURY
CHILDREN'S BOOKS
LONDON OXFORD NEW YORK NEW DELHI SYDNEY

BLOOMSBURY CHILDREN'S BOOKS
Bloomsbury Publishing Plc
50 Bedford Square, London WC1B 3DP, UK
29 Earlsfort Terrace, Dublin 2, Ireland

BLOOMSBURY, BLOOMSBURY CHILDREN'S BOOKS and the
Diana logo are trademarks of Bloomsbury Publishing Plc

First published in Great Britain in 2021 by Bloomsbury Publishing Plc

A catalogue record for this book is available from the British Library

ISBN: PB: 978-1-5266-0776-8; eBook: 978-1-5266-0777-5

2 4 6 8 10 9 7 5 3 1

Printed and bound in Great Britain by CPI Group (UK) Ltd,
Croydon CR0 4YY

To find out more about our authors and books visit www.bloomsbury.com
and sign up for our newsletters

For the Milway family:
Alex, Katie, Cecily & Hetty

1

Hunter and Prey

'We'll never do it!' moaned Gobkin. He threw his spear down into the quagmire of dirt, hair and congealed fat surrounding his feet, where it landed with a dull *splot* sound. 'It's *hopeless.*'

Gafferty Sprout counted down from five in her head. She looked at her little brother, his scared face criss-crossed with shadows cast by the grille that covered the extractor pipe in which they were hidden. Warm, greasy light oozed through the metal lattice and dribbled gleaming spots on to the lenses of Gobkin's goggles. Or was that the glistening of his frightened tears?

Be patient with him, Dad had said to her before the two of them had set out on the expedition. *He's young, but he must learn our ways*. Gafferty was learning more about Gobkin's ways, so far. Annoying little snivel-scrap! He'd moaned and whined all the way through the tunnel. He'd griped and groaned as they scaled the wall to get to the pipe. He'd grumbled and groused as they squeezed through the conveniently sized hole cut in its side. He'd carped and bellyached as they passed the now useless fan that Dad had carefully detached on a previous visit. It was Gobkin's first time properly out in the Big World and he was acting like it was bath night!

Dad had taken Gafferty out on her first hunt. She'd been brave. The oldest child had to be brave. If something happened to Mum or Dad, then she would be the one in charge. Gobkin was different. He was three years younger than Gafferty, and Mum and Dad had spoilt him, protected him. But that had all changed six months ago, when their little brother, Grub, had been born. A creature of snot and bad temper, he now took up all their parents' time. Gobkin was no longer the youngest. Gobkin needed to grow up.

Gafferty sighed irritably. This would be a lot easier if he weren't so much younger than her. But then, she had never known anyone of her own age. It was a constant annoyance, not having anyone who understood what she was feeling. Almost as much of a constant annoyance as Gobkin. Her hands toyed anxiously with the strap of her scavenger bag. The truth was that she was feeling nervous, and having a miserable, insecure assistant with her made it worse.

'I've done this a hundred times, you fimbling grizzle-head!' she said finally, summoning the effort to sound confident. 'Well, once or twice. Even three or four times. Lots of times. Maybe.'

'And Dad was with you then.'

'Don't worry, Gob. It'll be easy. I know what I'm doing.' She peered through the grille at the activity taking place in the noisy kitchen on its other side. 'And I have our prey in my sights.'

Gobkin leaned forward, his curiosity getting the better of him.

'Where … ?' he began.

Without warning, a shadow fell over the grille.

'Humans!' hissed Gafferty. She threw her arms protectively around her brother and dragged him backwards through the muck. They crouched in the darkness, frozen with fear, trying not to breathe in the rancid stench of their surroundings.

A gigantic eye stared through the grille. Gobkin

squealed and even Gafferty gave a sharp intake of breath. The eye frowned, blinked, then disappeared. Before the children had time to act, an enormous finger, wider and taller than either of them, rammed against the grille, sending a rattling echo down the pipe. Gafferty and Gobkin covered their ears as the finger hit the metal mesh once more.

'Oi, Barry!' boomed a voice. 'Is this extractor broken again?'

'Aye, boss,' called Barry, from somewhere in the kitchen. 'Keeps getting fixed, keeps getting broken. Mice, I reckon.'

'Mice?' snapped the boss. 'Got screwdrivers, have they? Don't let anyone hear you talk about mice, or we'll be closed down.' The voice grew quieter. The giant was moving away from the pipe. 'And where would we be without McGreasy's Burgers? Where would everyone go for their chips then, eh?'

'I don't think I'll ever get used to Big Folk,' whispered Gobkin, getting to his feet and reaching for his spear, 'with their great big stomping feet and humongous bottoms wobbling about overhead. And always shouting about everything! Why can't everyone be like us? Smidgens. Too small to cause any trouble ...'

4

'But big enough to care.' Gafferty finished their dad's often-repeated adage. She saw Gobkin's eyes shine as his brain caught up.

'Chips,' he said. 'They're making *chips*.'

'Chips,' confirmed Gafferty, nodding. 'Our prey. Golden, plump and crispy, completely defenceless, and ours for the taking. That's what we're hunting today. One chip will do nicely for dinner for all of us.'

'And don't forget the *kurrisorce*,' said Gobkin, drooling slightly. 'I read about it in *The Big Book of Big Folk Facts*. Humans love *kurrisorce*. The book says it channels the power of the mythical Kurri, god of chips.'

Gafferty smiled. That was more like it. Gobkin always had his nose in a book. Sometimes he talked like one. And now that he had survived a risky encounter with the Big Folk, his hunger was making him bolder. They pressed their faces against the grille and stared out at the Big World.

Rule One of the Smidgens: *stay hidden and observe*. From inside the extractor fan they could watch the goings-on of the burger bar. There were two chefs – Barry and his boss – cooking the burgers and sausages on the griddle, and frying chips, nuggets and anything else anyone cared to batter and fry in a deep vat of boiling oil.

Dealing with humans – who were at least twenty times as tall as you – was a dangerous business for all manner of reasons. If you weren't dodging human feet, then there were human-made death-traps. You could easily end up as a Smidgen-fritter if you weren't careful.

A counter separated the kitchen from the shop, where customers waited for their orders. Gafferty had chosen a quiet time for the hunt when the cooks were preparing food in readiness for the evening rush. There were no customers, and that meant fewer eyes to see them.

'It's time,' she said. 'Let the hunt begin.'

2

Into the Frying Pan

Rule Two of the Smidgens: *don't do anything flipping stupid*. That was easier said than done.

'Get the rope out,' Gafferty said, taking command. Whilst Gobkin rummaged obediently in his pack for a coil of stolen fishing line, she made last-minute adjustments to her scavenger suit.

Pulling on a couple of laces on either side of her waistcoat, she drew out four tubes of material from hidden pockets so that they dangled freely about her, making it look like she had grown extra arms. Then she drew her hood over her short red hair, a hood spotted with velvet eyes. Her clothes were a soft grey colour, like that of the spider she was meant to resemble. Admittedly, she was quite big for a spider, just as Gobkin was quite big to be the fly that formed his disguise, with his goggles and wing-shaped backpack and furry leggings, but the Smidgens never intended for themselves to be seen at all. *It's in case someone catches a glimpse of you from the corner of their eye*, as Mum said. *If the Big Folk see a shape that they think they recognise, they won't bother looking too closely.*

All Sprout family members picked their creepy-crawly guise at a young age and, once decided, stayed loyal to it. Dad was a beetle, Mum was a ladybird and Grub was – appropriately, given the amount of slime he produced – a slug. At least for now. Gobkin had toyed with being a grasshopper for a while, but had decided on a housefly, for their speed and dexterity. And he said they had a fascinating way of digesting their food, which had sounded disgusting to Gafferty when Gob had described it to them in detail at the dinner table.

With her bag slung round her shoulder, Gafferty was finally ready. Gobkin handed her the rope.

'Let's get this over with,' he said, biting his lip.

Gafferty flicked the catch on the grille (another bit of Dad's handiwork, along with the hinges that turned the metal grid into a door) and carefully pulled it open. The

two cooks were busy at the
griddle, their backs turned to
the chip fryer. The coast was clear. Gafferty
secured one end of the rope around a rivet
poking up from the floor of the pipe. She
let the remainder drop into the heavy,
oily air of the kitchen.

It was a short but nervous climb
down from the extractor fan. They
touched ground on a box of plastic gloves that
sat on a shelf beneath the pipe, along with
supplies of sauce, mayonnaise and mustard.
As they paused for breath behind a
ketchup bottle, Gafferty said: 'Mum
uses those gloves to make waterproof
clothing. I could stuff one into my bag
on the way back, but I don't want to make
things too complicated. We're here for the
chips. Carrying too much will slow us down.'

Gobkin nodded.

'Rule Three of the Smidgens: *be ready to
run, and run fast*,' he recited.

They scurried along the shelf
to its end. Then it was just a

quick jump into a soft pile of paper napkins that were heaped on the kitchen counter below, followed by a short dash across the counter to the deep fat fryer, its oil boiling with the menace of a restive volcano. They'd almost made it!

A bell chimed through the shop. Gobkin looked at his sister in alarm.

'The door!' hissed Gafferty. 'There's a customer! That's all we need.'

They dived into the shadow of a large salt shaker sitting next to the fryer. Gafferty peeped around its curved edge. It was a boy, barely visible behind the glass countertop, its surface misted with steam. One of the human cooks lumbered over from the griddle. It was Barry, judging from his voice.

'And what can I do for you, young lad?' he said, leaning over the counter to greet the customer.

'Small portion of chips, please,' said the boy, too busy picking his nose to pay attention to anything else.

'Coming up,' said Barry in reply. 'You're in luck – there's a batch just about ready.'

He turned to the fryer, his shadow plunging Gafferty and Gobkin's hiding place into darkness. They cowered behind the salt shaker, Gafferty's heart thumping like a drum in her chest. Next to her, Gobkin gripped his spear tightly to stop himself from shaking with terror. She put her hand on his shoulder to reassure him – he mustn't lose his nerve now! But what could they do? The human was bound to see them if they stayed here!

Barry took a sheet of greaseproof paper and laid it on the counter next to the salt shaker. The edges of the paper curled upwards. It gave Gafferty an idea, a risky one, but it might save them. Rule Four of the Smidgens: *if in doubt, make it up!*

The cook lifted the metal basket of chips from the fryer, shaking it to drain the excess oil. Using a large scoop, he shovelled a portion on to the paper. Globules of hot fat spat from the golden pile of fried potato, one fizzing dangerously close to Gobkin's ear.

'I want to go home!' he squeaked.

Gafferty grabbed his arm. She knew what was about to happen next.

'Get ready to run,' she whispered.

As she expected, Barry turned to the chip buyer.

'Would you like them salted?' he said.

Gafferty didn't wait to listen for the reply.

'Now!' she hissed. She dragged Gobkin away from the salt shaker and dived beneath the curl of the chip paper.

They crawled on their bellies under its cover, sweating in the heat radiating from the freshly cooked food sitting on its surface. Gobkin had just pulled his foot out of view when Barry turned back and reached for the shaker that had been their hiding place moments before. Salt hailed over the chips, rattling on to the paper above their heads. Her elbows hurting with effort, Gafferty wriggled across to the far side where the chip wrapper brushed up against a huge tub of margarine. Again, she waited for the moment when she knew Barry's back would be turned.

'And vinegar?' she heard him ask the hungry customer. That was it! She jumped up and scrambled behind the tub, pulling Gobkin along with her. The two of them sank to their knees, panting for breath.

Vinegar showered over the chips nearby. Gafferty grabbed the spear that Gobkin still clutched tightly. She'd not forgotten why they were there. Barry was now folding up the paper into a neat package, spinning it around as he tucked in the corners. He'd had so much practice he could make the creases in the wrapper without looking, something that Gafferty planned to use to her advantage. As the half-finished parcel of food turned towards them, she stabbed the nearest chip with lightning speed, a spider ambushing its victim, and hauled it free. Gobkin, who had watched with amazement, helped her drag it into their hiding place.

'And that,' said Gafferty, grinning as her brother eyed their still-warm, golden prize, 'is what I call a takeaway.'

3

Terror in the Tunnel

Getting the chip back home would be just as risky, but Gafferty and Gobkin were in luck. After the boy had left, Barry returned to cooking duties at the griddle, entering into a long discussion with his boss about the previous evening's football scores. They didn't notice the odd sight of an unusually large spider tearing off a corner of paper to wrap up a single chip. Or using string to fasten the little parcel to its back like a piece of luggage, helped by a remarkably large fly. The strange creatures then clambered up on to the shelf and shinned up a piece of thread hanging from the open extractor fan, before disappearing inside. Barry and his boss didn't notice, but someone else did.

A woman, serene and unsmiling, stood outside the shop, staring in through the window. She was tall and imposingly athletic, smartly dressed in a long black velvet coat over a smoke-grey suit. Her dark hair was swept up into a neat bun, and she wore a necklace of large glass beads that clinked gently as she moved. Her eyes, though hidden by sunglasses, were trained to spot the unusual. Passing the shop on her way to the hotel, pulling a suitcase-on-wheels behind her, she had seen the boy with his unhygienic fingers buying the parcel of chips. Nothing unusual about that – boys were *always* unhygienic in her experience – but it was the blink-and-you'd-miss-it activity of the peculiar little bug people that had got her attention. Claudia Slymark was also a hunter, and she was hunting Smidgens.

'That's a bit of good fortune,' she said to herself.

'I suppose they have to get food from somewhere,' said a voice. It was a cold sound, with a slight echo, as if the speaker were talking from inside a bathroom.

'I like insects,' said another voice. 'Cockroach sandwiches are very tasty if you remember the ketchup.'

'Spiders aren't insects,' Claudia said in reply, though there was no one there. 'Anyway, we don't need to *like* them. Or eat them.'

'Yet,' persisted the second voice.

'We just need to catch one,' said Claudia firmly.

'Shall I follow, Miss Slymark?' asked a third voice, hungrily.

Claudia nodded. Her long fingers went to her necklace. She pulled at one of the beads and it came away from the chain – it wasn't a bead but a small bottle, attached to the necklace by its stopper. 'But don't go far. I don't want you to dissipate.'

There was a growl of frustration from the bottle, and a rush of air from its neck. It formed a misty shape that slid under the door of the shop and into the extractor pipe, rustling the pile of napkins as it passed.

'Hinchsniff is too eager,' said the first voice, tutting with disapproval from another bottle. 'He's like a dog after a rabbit in its burrow.'

Gafferty and Gobkin scampered through the tunnel, their steps buoyed by their triumph at McGreasy's. They'd forgotten to get the precious *kurrisorce* and Gobkin had left his spear behind somewhere, but that didn't matter (although Gafferty was sure Gobkin would complain about both later). The expedition had been a success and there was a freshly cooked chip for dinner.

'Wait till Mum and Dad hear what happened!' said Gobkin, running a little ahead of his sister, who was burdened with their trophy on her back. 'Did you see how I dived under that paper?' He made a dramatic but awkward leap, the matchstick torch he carried to light their way sputtering with the sudden movement. Gafferty laughed.

'They'll be very proud of you,' she said. 'But leave out some of the more exciting details. You know how they worry.'

Gobkin frowned. 'Hmmm,' he said, gloomily. 'I suppose so.' Then his face brightened. 'Hey – do you remember that huge worm we passed on the way to the shop? Mum's been teaching me about how they eat earth then poo out compost for the plants! Did you know? I wonder if it's still there.'

He raced off down the tunnel, leaving Gafferty in the dark.

'Wait!' she called. 'Forget your silly worm, I can barely see!' But he was gone.

She remembered there was a light-stone in her bag. The veins of phosphorescence that ran through the pebble generated enough of a glow for her to find her way, although its green radiance was slightly eerie. She hung it by its string around her neck and flinched as the cold stone touched her skin. Then a deeper chill ran through her, but it wasn't the stone's fault: the temperature in the passageway had dropped. How could that be? There were never any breezes in the tunnels. They were usually quite stuffy, if anything. She stopped, suddenly nervous. She felt like she was being watched.

'Gobkin?' she called into the darkness, her voice sounding weak and lost in the emptiness. 'Gob – are you there?'

A sound close to her ear: a murmur, a breath; it played through her hair and touched her cheek. It was saying something, laughing at her. She gasped and staggered back in horror. Something – something creepy – was in the tunnel with her.

'Who's … who's there?'

The shadow moved like liquid. Whatever it was, it was circling her, as if she were being inspected or sized up for some purpose. She spun around, trying to catch sight of it. Her hand trembled as she stretched out to grab hold of something, to make sense of the formless dark, but at the same time fearing what it might find. Stumbling, the weight on her back unbalanced her and she fell with a bump to the ground, crushing one end of the chip into the earth.

'Get away!' she cried, clawing at the air in panic.

But the air just laughed, shaping and reshaping into inky, menacing silhouettes. They came together as a huge, shadowy hand that lunged forward and wrapped her in its cold, sinister fingers.

4

The Door in the Dark

'Helpless, pitiful little creature,' the monster hissed as it surrounded her. 'Pathetic. What does she want with you? What does she want with something so … small? Far too small to be of any importance.'

Frost formed on Gafferty's hair, and she felt her body numbing with cold and terror. The thing was draining her resolve, dulling her senses. She wanted to give in to it. She was no match for whatever this malevolent creature was.

But … what if it finds Gobkin?

The thought of her little brother was the spark she needed. She was responsible for him! Her mind struggled against the oppressive, deadening presence. It seemed hopeless at first. Then she remembered Dad's saying.

She'd always thought it was soft, but it gave her hope.

'Too small to cause any trouble, maybe,' she blurted out, her voice getting stronger with each word, 'but big enough to care!' The frost melted, and Gafferty could feel her blood warm her from within, her thoughts clearing.

The thing hesitated, taken aback. The tiny girl had spirit – it had not expected that! It only paused for a moment, but it was enough time for Gafferty to roll out of its clutches, scramble to her feet and run.

She bolted down the tunnel. She couldn't lead it to Gobkin – what could she do? Gafferty scoured her brain for a solution. She remembered Rule Four: *if in doubt, make it up!* There was a fork in the tunnel ahead. The right-hand passage led home – Gobkin would have taken that. The left-hand passage led into the forbidden parts of the Tangle.

The Tangle: the vast network of tunnels that ran under the human town. It had once housed many Smidgens – their homes, their schools, their shops and markets, their communities. But now the Smidgens were gone, except for her little family, and all the old maps of the Tangle had gone with them. It was an unending, empty labyrinth, a setting for ghost stories to scare naughty Smidgen-kids

at bedtime. Dad had forbidden her to ever go beyond their known routes. *If you're not careful you could be lost for good*, he'd say. She knew she shouldn't go down there. But this was an emergency.

Without wavering she fled into the unwelcoming blackness. The thing swept after her, she could feel the cold air on her heels. It was too fast; she would never escape it – not carrying this weight! It was catching up, almost upon her!

Then the floor disappeared from under her feet.

For a split second she was running in empty space.

With a crash she landed on a bank of loose shingle, sending up a cloud of dust around her, her legs giving way in the pain and shock of the impact. The ground had collapsed into a crater and she was tumbling into it, her spider arms flailing ridiculously as she rolled over rocks and slid through drifts of grit and pebbles. She dug her fingers into the ground, bringing her fall to an abrupt halt, just before she slammed against a jagged rock.

Gafferty lay still for a minute, panting furiously. She tested her arms and legs, moving them gently. Nothing was broken, but there would probably be bruises in the morning. Then she thought: *the creature! What happened to it?*

She looked around, then back up to the tunnel. The thing leered down at her. The air swirled violently but the shape didn't move any nearer, though she sensed it desperately wanted to. Why didn't it come for her? It was as if an invisible wall had sprung up between them, holding it back. There was a tense pause as the creature appeared to decide what to do next. Then, with an exasperated snarl, the chill slowly retreated. Gafferty wanted to call out, to warn Gobkin, but she knew she mustn't draw him into the creature's path. She waited, listening for signs that it really had gone and frantically hoping that her brother wouldn't blunder into it by accident. Painful minutes passed but there was only silence. She breathed a long sigh of relief.

She wasn't out of the woods yet: there could be more dangers lurking in this unexplored warren. She carefully got to her feet, ready to run. Gafferty could see by the glow of the light-stone that she was in another tunnel that ran below the first. At some point the roof had fallen in, joining the two tunnels together. The lower tunnel stretched away into the darkness. And there, in the stone wall in front of her, a door. It was rather grand, framed by carved pillars and ornate but long-rusted metalwork, but the most important thing was its size. It was a door made for a Smidgen.

Gafferty couldn't resist. Dad wouldn't like it, but she had to know. What if it had been someone's home? A quick look and then she would go and find Gobkin.

She knew it was silly, but she knocked quietly, just in case. No answer. She leaned against the wooden surface and pushed. The door resisted for a second then opened with a complaining rasp. The room beyond was large, its walls lined with empty shelves, laden with dust. Perhaps it had been a library, once filled with books. Clearly no one had been here for a long time. Gafferty wasn't surprised but couldn't help but be disappointed.

She turned to leave, then something caught her eye. The shelves weren't quite empty. A solitary forgotten book lay forlornly on a bottom shelf. Gafferty picked it up.

The cover was soft, not much more than a piece of cloth. There were three symbols on it, the first a kind of triangular shape like a pyramid, followed by a circle, followed by an upside-down triangle. It didn't look like a storybook. And it wasn't: opening the cover, Gafferty was faced with bold letters announcing the book was an atlas.

A Map of the Tangle, it said. *Showing All the Secret Roads and Lost and Legendary Ways of the Three Clans. In Case We Forget*. A map of the Tangle – this was almost better than finding treasure! She quickly stuffed the book into her bag and made her way back out into the tunnel.

A spot of light shone from overhead. It was Gobkin's torch. She saw his worried face looking down at her from the upper passageway.

'Gafferty?' He was anxious, but unharmed. 'Why are you down there? It's not allowed.' He gawped at her dust-spotted face as she scrambled back up the rockfall. 'Are you OK? You're covered in dirt and scratches.'

'Yes. I'm – I'm fine.' No need to frighten Gobkin. She glanced around at the dancing shadows. The tunnel was deserted apart from the two of them. 'I took a wrong turn and fell down this hole, that's all.

That's what happens when you run off like that, leaving me without a light to show the way. Don't ever do that again, hasty-toes!'

'All right!' said Gobkin, grumpily. 'I was only asking. You won't get me into trouble, will you?'

'No.' Her voice softened. This wasn't his fault really. 'No, I won't tell.' And anyway, thanks to him she had found the atlas, a relic of another time. It was important. It was going to change things.

'Good,' he said, brightening. 'Anyway, the worm had gone if you're interested. Can we go home? I'm so hungry I could eat the whole chip myself, including the paper. Though how you're going to explain why it's so squashed and dirty, I've no idea.'

5
The Unusual
Claudia Slymark

Claudia lounged on a bench a little way down the street from the burger bar, her beautiful face crumpled with displeasure. There had been nothing else to do while she waited for Hinchsniff to return, and curiosity had got the better of her, so she'd bought a portion of chips from a surprised Barry. Elegant and well-manicured, she was not his usual sort of customer. Claudia was not a usual sort of person by any measurement. She was accustomed to the finer things in life: dining in the most expensive restaurants and eating the best cuisine cooked by the most talented chefs. Not sitting in the street eating chips in curry sauce, cooked by a ketchup-splattered oaf from McGreasy's. The paper parcel lay open in her lap, its contents spread out like the entrails of a dissected carcass.

'Are they tasty, Miss Slymark?' enquired Totherbligh, from the green bottle on her necklace. 'Crispy, with just a light sprinkling of salt?' Although her seekers – as she called them – didn't eat, they seemed to enjoy seeing others experience food. The memory of it had stayed with them long after they had finished having a use for it.

'No,' said Claudia, between chews. 'They're cold and soggy and are so over-salted my lips are shrivelling up like a pair of slugs. I don't know what people see in them.' She hadn't even attempted the curry sauce. It reminded her too much of a chalice of fermented corpse juice she

had stolen from the Bucharest Museum of Antiquities. It had fetched a good price from the League of Necromancy, enough to buy her the apartment in New York, but it was not something she would choose to pour on her dinner.

'Slugs!' said Peggy Gums, enthusiastically, from the pink bottle. 'Now, there's a snack. Yummy!'

Totherbligh sniffed in disgust.

Claudia smiled. Her seekers were quite different from one another. It was what had made them so useful up until now. Hinchsniff, wild and unpredictable but cunning. Totherbligh, pompous and jolly but sneaky. And Peggy Gums, who was just plain barmy but also a little bit frightening.

However, Claudia was very much in charge. After all, she was the one who had 'liberated' them, as she put it, from their confinement in the high-security bank vault in Zurich. It had been an interesting moment in her career, a career that already had more than its fair share of interest.

She had started as an ordinary thief, a cat burglar. She could climb a wall quickly and silently, her limbs muscular and elastic and her grip strong and unyielding. She had become an expert at crowbarring, lock-picking and safe-cracking. And most importantly, not once had she left a trace of a clue and she had *never* been caught. Her escapades had baffled and dumbfounded police and detectives all over the world.

It was this reputation for discretion that had brought her to the attention of the shadowy supernatural underworld. Objects of magic were extremely valuable, and some people would go to any lengths to hide them away, and even greater lengths to obtain them. Warlocks and sorcerers, necromancers and witches – in short, the *wrong* sort of magical people – sought out her services. Enchanted artefacts were often protected by safes and keys and bars of iron, a metal that resisted any spells but not Claudia's skills.

The existence of magic was a surprise to her, but she soon adjusted and even picked up some knowledge along the way. It was when she met the ghosts – as that's what the seekers were – that her career really began to take off.

She had been after a cursed dagger worth millions of dollars, but the vault was an Aladdin's cave of treasures, magical and otherwise. In the brief time she had before the guards realised the safe door was open, it would have been impossible to find the dagger amongst the pile of scrolls and amulets and crystal orbs – were it not for the ghosts. They had whispered its location to her from their bottles, which sat in a row on a dusty shelf like the perfume counter of a forgotten shop.

'Take us with you!' they had called. They weren't part of the plan, but Claudia had known instantly the ghosts could be helpful. She had made room for them in her bag, next to the dagger. One favour in return for another.

A spell, cast by their original owner, a warlock of sorts, bound each of the seekers to their glass prisons. They could wander a certain distance, under doors or through keyholes – places that a very much alive and solid thief like Claudia couldn't go. If they went beyond the limits set by the spell, they would evaporate into nothingness. They acted as spies or scouts and were even capable of a little light-fingered work themselves – in fact, there were no fingers lighter. Claudia didn't care about their long-finished life stories or why they had been imprisoned – they were her tools, business employees at best. But they seemed quite happy. Claudia travelled the world and did all sorts of curious and not very legal things, and the ghosts enjoyed the ride. The Exploding Emerald of Rajpur, the Golden Komodo of Sumatra, the Gossiping Skull of Kiev, the Invisible Cat of the Pharaoh Semerkhet – Claudia and the seekers had pinched them all and earned a lot of money (and a few scratches) in the process.

Their latest assignment was different. Claudia had received a letter.

FIND THE SMIDGENS, it read, in a strange, forced handwriting. FIND OUT WHAT THEY KNOW OF THE MIRROR OF TROKANIS. IF YOU DISCOVER ITS WHEREABOUTS, I WILL PROVIDE ANY RICHES YOU DESIRE.

Claudia was intrigued. Most letters begged for her assistance. This one demanded it. There was no name, just a post office box number for replies. Claudia liked a mystery. She accepted the job.

On her trips around the world, she took the opportunity to scour libraries and book collections and museums, sometimes bribing, sometimes stealing, searching for stories of Smidgens. Frustratingly, information was patchy, but Claudia did eventually discover two facts.

Firstly, the Smidgens were tiny people who kept out of the way of their huge human cousins. Secondly, they had been numerous once, particularly in this little town on the edge of a loch, nestled between a mountain and a forest. But there had been no sightings for years for some reason, and it was believed the little people might even be extinct. Claudia thought the town was worth investigating and couldn't quite believe her good fortune in sniffing out not just one but two Smidgens shortly after her arrival! She was eager to know what her seeker had learned.

She didn't have to wait too long. The ghost seeped out of McGreasy's, carrying with him the stale smell of chip fat and vinegar, and sullenly coiled his smoky form into the amber-coloured bottle next to the others.

'And?' Claudia said, impatiently.

'I lost them.' Hinchsniff was sulking. 'There's a whole network of tunnels down there. I could have followed them further if it weren't for the binding spell, Miss Slymark.'

'Did you learn anything useful?'

'They've got gumption. Any human would have crumpled under the effects of my fright-freeze. You're going to have a fight on your hands getting anything from the Smidgens.'

Claudia wasn't afraid of a challenge.

'Is that all you found?' she said.

A small stick-like object flew out of the bottle and landed on top of the uneaten chips. She wrinkled her nose in distaste.

'A toothpick? And a used one by the look of it.'

'It belonged to one of them,' chuckled Hinchsniff. 'He

was using it as a spear but left it behind. Very careless.'

Behind her sunglasses, Claudia's eyes glowed as she stoppered Hinchsniff's bottle.

'Very careless,' she agreed. She put the stick into her bag. Then, with perfect aim, she threw the unfinished food parcel over her shoulder and into a bin behind her. 'Time to check into our hotel room, I think. We have work to do ...'

6

At Home with the Sprouts

The Tangle was a mixture of different structures: some were simple channels carved through rock, like the way to McGreasy's. Others were old animal burrows or naturally formed caves and hollows. They had names dating back years, to a time when the tunnels were busy, well-lit thoroughfares: Forager's Way, The Quick Road, Hidden Lane, Behind-the-Market Street. They also regularly intersected with the world of the Big Folk.

'Put the torch out, Gob,' said Gafferty, as their path steadily climbed towards daylight. It was the last stretch before home – and potentially the most dangerous.

The tunnel ended in a roughly hewn doorway. Gafferty and Gobkin cautiously peered out from its shelter. A vast factory floor lay before them, noisy with Big Folk and their machinery: gurgling vats of boiling syrup, taps that poured dollops of coloured sugar into moulds, rattling conveyor belts carrying brightly decorated boxes. It was a chocolate factory – another hunting ground of the Smidgens. They had no shortage of fudge and jelly sweets in the larders at home. The entrance to the Tangle was just a mousehole in one of its walls, as far as the humans were concerned.

As soon as she thought it was safe, Gafferty signalled to Gobkin to run. The young Smidgens skirted the edge of the factory, darting under moving trolleys and dodging busy footsteps.

'Quickly!' Gafferty had to gripe at her brother more than once. 'Pay attention to where you're going, Gob, you dizzy scatter-wit!' He was so easily distracted by all the sweets passing by, and the many wonderful smells and mechanical sounds. He could be spotted by the Big Folk, or worse: not spotted and flattened by the giant tusked metal monster they called a forklift.

'Stop nagging,' said Gobkin. 'What's put you in such a bad mood?'

'You!' she snapped. 'How did I get stuck looking after an empty-headed little worry-bug?'

Gobkin muttered something to himself but kept close to her anyway.

They reached the old broken pipe near the stairwell at the back of the factory that they used as a slide into the basement. Gafferty shoved Gobkin down it, then sent the chip after him, before following them both. In the basement, behind a forgotten pile of boxes, there was an iron gate that guarded an entrance in the stone wall. A rusty sign saying **DO NOT ENTER** was fixed to its bars. Ignoring the warning, the Smidgens slipped underneath the gate and followed a passage that led to a large cave.

Here stood the home of the Sprout family, and it was rather a grand home for just the five of them. It was more like an entire tower block carved into a wall of rock. Hundreds of windows were cut through the stone, windows for hundreds of rooms.

Once, long before Gafferty was born, the rooms had been filled with Sprouts, with Dustyheads, Glowblossoms, Pickety-Pocketys and their relatives and friends, and the House of the Smidgens was known for its laughter, light and life, a hive abuzz with activity and noise. At least, it was according to Mum and Dad, who were told so by their parents. Now, only a few of the rooms were occupied and the remainder were filled with nothing but silence.

Some still had their furniture and fittings, dust-heavy objects whose owners had long since departed.

Gafferty and Gobkin's parents, Gumble and Gloria, had claimed part of the building's middle floors for the family: a cosy kitchen, two bathrooms, three bedrooms and a workshop, as well as a few storage rooms and larders. It was an island of life in the dead house. Heat, light and water were borrowed from the factory, thanks to cabling and pipes they had fashioned. Mum and Dad were experts in all things technical or mechanical, customising found, broken or stolen items from the Big World for their family's use. That only left the food to be scavenged, and hunting was increasingly the responsibility of the children.

Dad was the first to notice their arrival, as they staggered up the stairs and into the kitchen.

'Here's dinner!' he said. Gafferty saw him take in the dust on her clothes and the marks on her face and hands, and hide his concern under a smile. He rose from the kitchen table, where he was wrestling with the wiring in a lamp, reincarnated from an old Christmas tree light. A slab of a man, hair red like Gafferty's, he spread his freckled forearms around his son, obviously relieved to see them both back safely.

'All good?' He raised an eyebrow at Gafferty over Gobkin's shoulder, the simple question covering all manner of parental worries. She smiled weakly.

'It was fine,' she said, hauling the parcel on to the table. 'The chip's had a few bumps along the way. Gobkin did well, once he stopped whining.'

'I didn't whine!' Gobkin immediately objected, before realising he was being let off lightly, and bit his tongue.

Mum appeared from a bedroom with Grub balanced on her hip. The child, wrapped in a human baby's sock, stared malevolently at his older siblings, a dollop of mucus swinging from his nose like a gleaming pendulum.

'That will do very nicely,' Mum said, eyeing the chip and running her free hand through Gobkin's brown hair, all frizz and curls like her own. She brushed the dirt off Gafferty's jacket and kissed her on the cheek. 'Well done, you two! Now, clean yourselves up and we'll eat.'

Gafferty dunked her hands in the bottle cap sink,

glancing around her at the familiar room. The kitchen was their main living space, where the family came together, and probably the place she had spent most of her life: eating, reading and drawing when she was younger, cooking, cleaning and washing clothes now she was older. The bundles of herbs hanging from the ceiling to dry, the tiles made from pieces of a broken willow pattern plate, the polished button dishes, the hollowed acorn storage jars, the matchbox dresser – it was all reassuringly familiar. But Gafferty was uneasy. Something had changed today: the frightening encounter in the tunnel, finding the atlas. She was seeing things differently.

She was hungry for food, but she was hungrier for answers. *In Case We Forget*. Those were the words written on the atlas. It sounded like a memorial, something you would write on a gravestone. The Big Folk had machines – *The Big Book of Big Folk Facts* called them *kamras* – that could instantly paint a picture of a person, a picture they could keep forever to remind them of a loved one. The Smidgens had nothing like *kamras* and *fotoes*. All the Smidgens that had gone before her, all the other Sprouts – their faces would never be seen again, she would never know what they looked like. There were no memorials, unless you counted empty rooms. Gafferty hadn't much questioned her parents about their family's history, but this sad book stirred her thoughts. Could they really be the last Smidgens in the world? And if they were the last ones, she wanted to know why.

7

A History Lesson

Mum dumped the wriggling baby in his father's arms. Pulling the dusty paper wrapper from the chip, she used a blade from a pencil sharpener to slice the greasy object like an oversized loaf of bread. She laid the chip slices on a square of tinfoil and shoved them into the candle-warmed oven to reheat.

'Plenty of leftovers!' she said, carrying the remainder of the chip into an adjoining larder. 'Almost too much, even for our hungry mouths.'

'Why aren't there more of us, Mum?' said Gafferty, collecting a stack of plates from the dresser and placing them on the table.

'You can't be wanting another brother or sister?' said

Dad, mildly horrified. Grub gurgled furiously from his father's lap, as if the idea of further rivals for his parents' attention was completely unthinkable.

'No! Definitely not! Two are enough trouble.' Gafferty gave Gobkin a look. He stuck out his tongue at her as he scrubbed his hands. 'More Smidgens. People of my *own* age. What happened to all the other families that lived here? And in the Tangle? You've never really spoken much about it.'

'Not much to tell,' said Dad under his breath. 'Nothing good, anyway.'

'I'm sorry, Gafferty love,' Mum said sadly. She rinsed a spring onion leaf under the water pump before shredding it into pieces. 'I know it's been hard for you, being the only one of your age.' She dried her hands and sat with her family at the table. 'There are tales, but it's difficult to know truth from tattle after all these years. We can't give you an honest answer if we don't know ourselves.' She looked at each of her children in turn and sighed. 'There *were* lots more Smidgens once – you can tell that from the size of the House alone.'

'There were lots of families – clans?' Gafferty trod carefully. If she told them about the atlas, she would have to tell them she'd disobeyed them and gone into the

45

forbidden part of the Tangle, leaving Gob all alone.

'I don't know anything about any clans,' Mum said. 'But Smidgens lived here and throughout the Tangle, like the humans in their town above. Maybe even beyond the Tangle. And they were properly civilised too, more so than the Big Folk. My old grandpa said they knew a bit of magic.'

'Magic?' said Gobkin, his eyes widening.

'Small magic for Small Folk,' Mum said, smiling.

'Nothing fancy, I shouldn't think, but some of the tales say the Smidgens got lazy and forgot how to live without their magic.'

'What happened?' said Gafferty impatiently. 'Where did everyone go?'

'We don't really know what happened. A big falling out, I was told. That's what happens when people have time on their hands. But whatever happened, it was bad. Bad enough for folk to want to forget it. Bad enough for people to not want to write it down. People leave out the bits of history they don't like, the bits that don't suit them. Either way, after the Disaster, the magic was gone, and the Smidgens had to learn to live without it. But they struggled, and struggled badly.'

'They'd gone soft,' said Dad, with a dismissive snort. 'Careless. They'd forgotten how to survive. And that's no good when you live amongst the Big Folk.'

'The magic protected the Smidgens from humans, supposedly,' said Mum. 'Anyway, they found out about us, even hunted us. Treated us like rats!' She shuddered. 'They were dark days. The Smidgens left the Tangle as the humans dug up parts of it to find us, and those that remained hid themselves away, here at the House, relearning old skills of foraging and scavenging. But for a long while there was little food, and fewer babies, fewer Smidgens.'

'But that was years and years ago,' said Gafferty. '*Hundreds* of years.'

'It was never the same again,' said Dad. 'Our kind never really recovered. Many Smidgens thought there was a better life to be had elsewhere and moved on. Others have followed over the years. Until only us Sprouts remain.'

'But why? Why didn't we go too?' Gafferty said. 'Why are we stuck here in this … this miserable tomb? It's just us and … ghosts.' She shivered uncomfortably as the memory of the *thing* in the tunnel returned. It couldn't have been a ghost, could it? One of the Tangle stories come true?

'Oh, Gafferty,' Mum said, getting up. 'Leave, when we've the young ones to look after? Don't be silly.'

She went to the oven, humming to herself. It was the sign she wanted to change the subject, sensing an argument brewing.

'We're stuck here, as you say, young lady, because this is our home,' said Dad, not taking the hint. Gafferty often battled with him, their stubbornness evenly matched. 'It's where we belong! The world is still dangerous for

Smidgens, even if the Big Folk have forgotten us now and leave us alone. Have we heard from those who've left? No. The Sprouts made the right decision, staying here, staying safe, and we should be grateful for it, Gafferty.' His voice was thunderous, but Gafferty persisted.

'I *am* grateful,' she said. 'But there must be more Smidgens out there, mustn't there?' She waved her hand in the general direction of the factory. 'Perhaps if we looked, we'd find them. What's the good of me teaching Gobkin or Grub all the Smidgen-lore if we're the last? What's the point, Dad?'

'The point is *survival*,' her father said, rapping his big fist on the table so that the plates rattled. 'You want to go out searching for Smidgens in the Big Folks' world? You want freedom? It comes with a high price.'

'Prices are fine if something's worth it!' snapped Gafferty. 'And any price would be worth it to get away from here!'

'Gafferty!' Mum turned from the oven, her voice filled with hurt, her eyes with sadness. Gafferty's face burned red in anger and shame. She got up from the table and ran out of the room, out into the darkness of the abandoned House. She had never felt more alone.

8

The Glass Knife

Voices crowded her mind – angry, frustrated and resentful voices – as she wandered through the shadowy corridors. Gafferty was cross with her parents, and cross with herself for being cross. She loved Mum and Dad deeply and knew they loved her, of course. So why couldn't she help feeling she had to escape from the life she shared with them? There was a voice of fear too. What was out there in the Big World? And worse: what if she never got the chance to see it? It was all so maddening!

The House had been her playground once. Each room triggered a memory as she passed through it. The games she had played: hide-and-seek with a colony of house spiders on the fifth floor, bowling in a long hallway on the third. Under an enormous dining table on the second floor she found the remains of a den, the paper napkin tent she had made still in place, yellowed and crumpled.

She had been content in her own company then, thinking nothing of the lack of other folk. But now the sad, neglected spaces bothered her, their emptiness cruelly mirroring her loneliness. She needed the company of others of her own age. The occasional abandoned shoe or forgotten toy were all that remained of the Smidgen-lads and -lasses who had once made this place their home. Reminders of all the friends she'd been denied the chance to have. As she moved aimlessly through the building, Gafferty found the quiet hurt her ears. This place needed to come alive! The House should be full once more.

'I have to find other Smidgens,' she said aloud. 'I *have* to.'

Not quite ready to go back to face her family and apologise, she walked some more, upstairs and down, through box rooms, bedrooms and cellars, gradually shedding her bad temper and uneasy thoughts like discarded clothes. Some rooms were in complete darkness, some lit by distant second-hand light borrowed from the stairwells of the Sprout home, but Gafferty could find her way around by touch, it was all so familiar. Her fingertips led her to a tool store where her parents had put some of her old playthings, to keep them safe from her brothers' rough hands. She needed to see objects that reminded her of a time when she had fewer cares. To her surprise, she found Dad there, brooding silently in the glow of a light-stone. He was sharpening the end of a toothpick, presumably to replace Gobkin's lost spear.

'You've missed your dinner,' he said, without looking at her.

There was an expectant silence. Mum usually did the peacemaking, Dad's bluntness often making speeches awkward. Gafferty realised how tired he seemed; how worn both her parents were. Keeping a family happy without any outside help must be such hard work. It didn't help when the oldest child stormed off in a tantrum. She winced at the recollection.

'I'm sorry,' she said quietly, grabbing his hand and giving it a squeeze. Dad put down the spear and gave her a clumsy hug.

'You're getting older, flexing your wings,' he said. 'Your mum – both of us – we want to keep you tucked up in the nest a while longer, that's all. Doesn't mean you can't have adventures.'

Gafferty's thoughts went to the atlas. It was too soon

to mention it. Exploring the Tangle – that would be an adventure too far for her parents. It would have to remain her secret for now. Dad continued:

'What's important is that you keep your brother from harm, and yourself too. Until Grub's more independent and less of a wriggling little sack of bile, we need to pull together and help each other out. Gobkin needs to do his bit, like the rest of us. And we need you to keep an eye on him and teach him everything you know. Pass on the Smidgens' knowledge. There's plenty of time to follow your dreams. Just not now, eh?'

He was trying to see her side. Gafferty felt a twinge of guilt. She was keeping things from him.

'There was … something in the tunnel today,' she began. 'Something bad. It came after me, but I got away from it. It didn't see Gobkin – he was safe. I don't know what it was, something magical perhaps, but I think it wanted me for something.'

Dad frowned.

'There's dark beasts in the heart of the Tangle, it's always been said. Things that wandered in and made a home for themselves, after the Disaster left it abandoned. But I've not seen anything so close to our usual paths.' He reached under a workbench and pulled out a metal box, an empty cat food tin with a cloth draped over it. The box rattled as he dragged it across the floor and pulled back the cover. It was filled with tools. No – not tools, Gafferty realised. These were weapons: swords, axes, daggers, with sharp metal blades and handles carved from wood or plastic. 'You might as well be protected,' Dad muttered. 'Though don't tell your mother.'

'Where did you get these?' Gafferty said, picking up a sword and trying its weight.

'I collected them from around the House and hid them. I didn't want you youngsters getting your hands on anything too dangerous before you were ready. Some are from the old times, probably. They'll have dealt with beasties like the one you met, maybe Big Folk too.'

Gafferty's fingers touched upon a smooth surface. It was a knife, but its thick blade was made of a rose-coloured glass, a strip of material wrapped around the blunt end as a grip.

'I don't remember seeing that before,' remarked Dad, as she held it up. 'Looks good and sharp too. Useful for all kinds of things.'

Despite being kept in the box for years, the glass had somehow stayed polished, and sparkled as if it had an inner light of its own. It had … a personality, Gafferty decided. It felt like it belonged in her hand. She smiled.

'This will do for me,' she said. 'This spider now has a bite.'

9

The Helpful Spider

Tucking the knife inside her jacket, Gafferty and her father made their way back to the Sprout kitchen. The washed pots and dishes from the meal were piled up by the sink, except for a single plate covered with a tea towel to keep its contents warm. Her dinner had been saved for her like she knew it would. Mum sat alone at the table, wrapped in her red shawl with its black ladybird spots, waiting.

'All sorted?' she said, eyeing them sternly.

Gafferty nodded silently and joined her at the table, tucking into the chip slice and chopped greens. The potato had gone soft, but she was so hungry she didn't care. Her mum stood and stooped to kiss her on the cheek: words weren't always necessary. Both parents relaxed. The argument over, life could go back to normal with everyone safe at home. But Gafferty knew that wasn't entirely true, and life wouldn't be the same. She had a map and she was going to use it to find other Smidgens.

She didn't look at the atlas again until the next morning. Mum let her have a lie-in, so she curled up in her bed, a cosy shelf cut into the stone wall of her room. With a mattress made from a washing sponge and covered with a quilt stuffed with feather barbs, moss and cotton wool, it was a snug spot for some reading. A money spider, about the size of her palm, had recently taken up residence in one corner of the bed nook, but it kept out of her way and she appreciated its mute company. Anyway, it was well known that spiders were good luck.

Gafferty flicked through the book, taking in all the detail.

'No wonder it's called the Tangle – it's more like a knot! Or as if a spider has spun a wonky web of ink over the paper.'

She laughed, although the spider didn't appear to be impressed by the idea and just stared at her with its many eyes. But it wasn't only the maps that had intrigued

Gafferty. She read the second part of the book's title again:

Showing All the Secret Roads and Lost and Legendary Ways of the Three Clans.

Mum said she hadn't heard of any clans of Smidgens before, but her parents didn't seem to know much about the past, about this great big Disaster, so that didn't mean an awful lot. The book was written by Smidgens for other Smidgens to use – that was clear from its size. And Smidgens lived in the Tangle so the Three Clans must be Smidgen clans, that was the only explanation! The Sprout family were probably one family amongst many that made up the clan.

'And just because our clan was stupid enough to die out or disappear, doesn't mean the other two did,' she said to the spider.

Her heart beat faster at the thought. She would make friends with other Smidgen-lads and -lasses when she found them. Friends her own age! She would share things with them, jokes, thoughts, ideas – things only another Smidgen would understand. What would it feel like to belong to something bigger than her family? She sighed wistfully then shook her head. She was getting carried away. She had to find them first – perhaps there was a clue in the atlas as to where they might be.

'Let's think about his logically,' Gafferty said.

First, she had to work out where the House, her home, was within the atlas's pages. It didn't take long to find. Whoever had created the book had drawn a little picture of it, with its many windows, and Gafferty recognised some of the paths leading away from it as those the Sprouts used in their scavenging trips. Next to the image of the House was a triangle.

'It's just like the triangle on the cover,' said Gafferty. 'I wonder if the three symbols are meant to stand for the three clans. Was the House the headquarters for one of them?'

She glanced up at the spider, but it wasn't going to help. It hadn't moved from its corner as it kept watch for reckless flies. Gafferty flipped through the pages, to see if she could find the other symbols.

'If one clan did live in the House,' she reasoned, 'the other clans might have had their own places to live in. If I find their symbol, I find their home.' She soon discovered one of the symbols, the upside-down triangle. It was drawn next to a picture of a tall, round tower, like that of a castle. There was nowhere like that nearby, as far as Gafferty knew. And there was more disappointment when she found the third symbol, the circle. It was beside a path that ran off the page with a question mark written by it. The path was labelled *To Parts Unknown*. That wasn't very useful. If the Smidgen who made the atlas didn't know where the third clan was, then she had no hope of finding it! She threw the open book on to the bed and sank back into her pillow.

'I give up, spider,' she said, but the creature had disappeared. Gafferty sat up and saw that while she had been reading, it had crawled down the wall and across the bedclothes and was slipping out of sight between the discarded atlas's pages. 'Be careful,' she said. 'I wouldn't want to trap you in the book accidentally.'

She gently lifted the page under which the spider was hiding. It scuttled out and sprang away, back up to its corner of the bed nook.

'Make up your mind!' said Gafferty, laughing. She looked down at the page in her hand. There were the three symbols, side by side, exactly as they were on the book's cover. She'd missed this!

'Well, well,' she said. 'Spiders are lucky, after all!'

The symbols were drawn next to a convergence of paths, which was labelled with the word *Smidgenmoot*. Gafferty didn't know what that meant, but it looked

important, as the word had been written larger than any other and underlined twice. And that wasn't all. There were drawings of places near to it that she knew, old Big Folk places like the market square.

It wouldn't be too difficult to work out where this Smidgenmoot was. And then ... then perhaps she could visit it! The thought was so daring it gave her a shiver. It could be her first little adventure, a voyage outside of her parents' world. She shook her head. No, she couldn't do it. Mum and Dad would be furious if they found out, going off by herself without telling them. But ... but they'd never know, would they? She'd never done anything so defiant before, but the more she thought about it the more certain she was it was something she had to do.

'Thank you, spider!' she said. 'An expedition of discovery! And who knows what – or *who* – I'm going to find?'

10

An Unplanned Excursion

For the rest of the morning, there were chores to be done: a hole in one of Gafferty's boots needed repairing using a strip of masking tape, Gobkin needed to be shown how to use spider silk to sew antennae on to his fly goggles, and bark chips needed chopping into pieces to fuel the boiler.

'We're running low on breadcrumbs,' Mum said as Gafferty walked into the kitchen with a bundle of bark. She was standing on a chair scrutinising a row of jars on the food shelf. 'And your father wants them to make cinnamon pudding. You can take Gobkin to the *kaffay* next to the factory after middle-meal. The cook in there always has a few spare crusts. Enough to keep us going for a while.'

Gobkin looked up from the table, where he was sat drawing a picture of an ant with a stub of red crayon.

'Can we get cake crumbs too?' he said eagerly.

'This afternoon?' said Gafferty. 'Do I *have* to?'

'Have you got other plans?' said her mother, raising an eyebrow as she rattled a jar labelled *Mustard Seeds*. 'Tea with the Queen of the Mountain Gnomes, perhaps?'

Gafferty bit her lip in annoyance. She did have other plans, as it happened. The Smidgenmoot – whatever it was – was waiting, and the last thing she wanted was to be a babysitter.

'I want to get cake!' whined Gobkin.

'Fine,' she said, dumping the bark chips in a box next to the boiler. She could do both – go exploring and get the stupid breadcrumbs. She would make this hunting trip a little more interesting.

At middle-meal, she found Gobkin at the kitchen table all ready and waiting, wearing his goggles and scavenger backpack. He was messily devouring potato waffles that Mum had made from some of the leftover chip.

'He's a keen lad when there's cake involved,' chuckled Dad, bouncing Grub on his knee. 'Listen, boy: enthusiasm is all well and good, but don't let it make you forget the dangers.'

'The specific dangers of a Big Folk *kaffay*,' recited Gobkin, spluttering potato everywhere, much to the delight of Grub, 'are boiling water, sharp knives and toasters. Also, beware of falling into sugar bowls.' *The Big Book of Big Folk Facts* was the foundation of all the Sprout family's knowledge of humans, supplemented by Great-Great-Uncle Flemm's *Manual for Surviving in the Big World, with Particular Attention to the Perils of Cats*, written by a distant relative of Dad's. Gobkin could quote whole pages.

Gafferty laughed. 'You've changed your tune since our visit to McGreasy's yesterday. We'll make a hunter of you yet.'

After finishing their food, Gobkin helped Gafferty get ready. They gathered on the table all the necessary items for an expedition. Fishing line for rope, bent pins for hooks, a bottle of water, a bundle of match-end torches with a lighting flint – and Gafferty's glass knife, which she fetched from its hiding place under her mattress. She'd avoided thinking about the strange encounter in the tunnel with the creepy *thing*, its awful, hungry coldness and what it might want with her. But the memory returned as she contemplated exploring the forgotten parts of the Tangle. What would she find there? Were

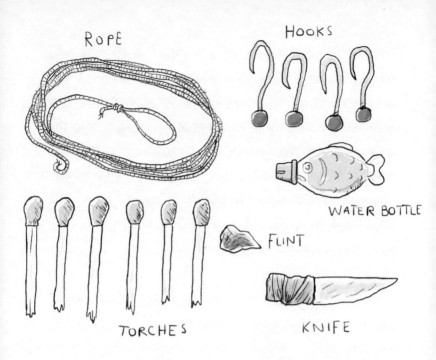

ROPE

HOOKS

WATER BOTTLE

FLINT

TORCHES

KNIFE

there other dangerous creatures lurking in the darkness? And was it somewhere she should be taking her little brother?

Whilst they packed, she studied the wallpaper plastered over the wall behind the table. It was, in fact, itself part of a map, a plan of the Big Folk town that Mum had rescued from a wastepaper bin, and it covered the space from floor to ceiling. Dad had written notes on to it of food sources and other useful scavenging places, as well as the locations of Tangle exits.

Mum and Dad were safely out of the way, giving an

enraged Grub a bath. Shrieks and splashes (from Grub) and curses (from Dad) emanated from the bathroom. Gafferty quickly fetched the atlas from her room and tried to match the location of the Smidgenmoot with the modern human landmarks. There was the humans' food market. The Smidgenmoot was close by, probably somewhere in that narrow alley that ran next to it. The atlas wasn't very clear on distances, but the Big Folk map was accurate, so it gave a better idea of how far away things were. Gafferty reckoned they could just about make it to the Smidgenmoot and then the *kaffay* without her parents noticing they had been gone too long.

'What's that?' asked Gobkin, pointing to the atlas.

'Nothing,' she said, hastily stuffing the book into her bag. 'Gob, as you're now so experienced, how do you fancy a little detour on our way to the *kaffay*? A test of our skills in navigation.'

'What do you mean?' Gobkin eyed her suspiciously. In his opinion, you didn't take detours when the quickest path led you to cake.

'Only a bit of exploring, that's all. Discovering new routes to places. You want to become as knowledgeable as me, don't you?'

Gobkin eyed her slyly.

'Do you want to go to the Smidgenmoot?' he said.

Gafferty was too surprised to pretend to look innocent.

'How did you know?' she said.

'I saw you gawping at it in that book. I'm not daft, Gafferty.'

'Hmmm, well … yes. Though I don't really know what it is.'

'A moot is a meeting, or a place to have a meeting,' Gobkin said nonchalantly. 'It's in Great-Great-Uncle Flemm's book. He talks about the Smidgens of the House having a moot to decide on important things. I thought you would have read his manual, what with you being so knowledgeable about everything.'

Gafferty flicked one of Gobkin's new antennae so that it wobbled about like a giddy flower.

'Don't be such a cheeky smarty-socks,' she said, although she was secretly pleased. A Smidgenmoot was a meeting of Smidgens! What better place to go searching for the other clans? Perhaps they were still meeting there. 'If you come on this little expedition I've in mind, and don't tell Mum and Dad, we'll get cake *and* I'll scavenge us some strawberry jam too.'

Gobkin looked unconvinced – he knew his father's opinions on exploring – but the promise of jam was too tempting. He nodded. Gafferty grinned. They slung their bags over their shoulders and scampered out of the House.

It wasn't long before they were crossing the packing area of the factory, where the boxes of sweets were stacked awaiting delivery. There was an entrance to the Tangle in a storeroom at its edge. They darted from stack to stack until they were in sight of the storeroom, then paused behind a pile of boxes as a young man appeared at its door.

'What's that thing he's pushing?' said Gobkin.

'It's called a *bysickal*,' said Gafferty, pleased to show her knowledge for a change. 'The Big Folk ride on them, making them move by flapping their feet. It's much faster than walking but not as fast as a *kar*. He must keep it in there.'

The man stopped and propped his bike against the boxes. Gobkin peered around to have a closer inspection of the unfamiliar contraption.

'You off home, Robbie?' said a woman, walking towards the man as he fastened his cycle helmet. She was clutching a bag of sweets and looking stressed.

'That's right,' said Robbie. 'My shift's done. Are you OK, Maureen?'

'The van left without this order of Fizzfires and

Rainbow Fudge for the corner shop on Market Street,' said Maureen. 'You couldn't drop it off on your way, could you? It'll save me a phone call and goodness knows how much paperwork.'

'Market Street!' whispered Gafferty. 'That's near where we want to go. He'll be there a lot sooner than us.' A thought forced its way into her mind, a dangerous, foolish thought, but she'd seemed to be making a habit of those lately.

'Do you—?' she began.

'No,' said Gobkin. 'I know what you're about to say, Gafferty, and I'm not doing it. You are never making me ride on that thing. Never!'

11

Map Reading

It had seemed a brilliant idea at the time, but Gafferty quickly regretted her decision to hitch a ride with Robbie. He was clearly in a hurry to get home, and not in the mood to do any favours for Maureen. As a result, he cycled as fast as he could through the twisty lanes of the town, the bike rattling over every bump in the road and hurtling around street corners at such a sharp angle he was almost horizontal.

The Smidgens, hidden in the panniers on the back of the bicycle, were flung around like two socks in a tumble dryer. Gafferty's stomach churned with every bounce but, surprisingly, Gobkin was having a whale of a time. She'd almost had to throw him on board, he was so

71

terrified, but once they'd got going, he discovered he had a taste for speed. For most of the way he was able to hang on to the bag's opening and peer out, watching the humans from under the shade cast by Robbie's sweaty bottom above, as the bike whizzed past them on its journey. He laughed gleefully at the sensation of the air rushing past his face. He'd never experienced anything like this before and loved every second.

'We should get *bysickals* of our own!' he yelled, as they zoomed down Hill Street, chased by a small yapping dog. It had spotted the tiny child peering out of the bag and dragged its owner along the road in its excitement. 'Do you think Mum and Dad could make them?'

'Not if your driving is as bad as Robbie's,' Gafferty replied, her face going green as she hung on to the sides of the pannier for dear life.

The bike braked suddenly, and they were hurled forward, Gobkin landing on top of his sister with a yelp.

'Get me out of here!' said Gafferty, furiously shoving Gobkin aside. 'I've had quite enough of Robbie the racer.'

They scrambled to the top of the bag and poked their heads out to find out where they were.

'It's Market Street,' said Gafferty. 'There's the corner shop. Quick, let's move whilst Robbie is delivering the sweets.'

There was a knot of anticipation in her stomach as they clambered out of the bag and ran across the pavement, hiding behind a drainpipe attached to the shop. The street was busy with shoppers. They'd have to be careful. Gafferty took the atlas out of her scavenger bag.

'Where's this moot thing, then?' said Gobkin, staring

73

at all the Big Folk walking by. 'Why are you so interested in it? And why are you keeping it a secret from Mum and Dad?'

'I'm looking for more Smidgens, Gob. Mum and Dad would worry that it might be dangerous. But wouldn't you like to have some Smidgen friends, instead of hanging around with your boring big sister all the time?'

Gobkin nodded, a little too readily for Gafferty's liking. She continued.

'I think the Smidgenmoot is where, long ago, three clans of Smidgens used to meet to talk about … I don't know, important Smidgen stuff. And perhaps some of them still do. It's worth a quick peek. Then we can go back to the *kaffay* and get the cake crumbs and jam.'

Gafferty's mind was alive with the idea of all those Smidgens meeting together in times past, all those voices – the discussions, the chatter, the laughter, the arguments! It must have been wonderful. She wished it could be like that again. She pictured herself walking into the moot, pictured the surprise on all the faces of the other Smidgens at seeing someone new! They would welcome her as one of their own, she was sure.

'And they came here, did they?' said Gobkin, looking around unsurely. 'To the middle of Market Street?'

Next to him, Gafferty scrutinised the atlas whilst simultaneously trying to remember the pattern of the kitchen wallpaper.

'No, of course not. If I'm reading this right, they met somewhere in –' she grabbed his hand and dragged him along the street, turning into a narrow alley, and then further until they were hidden in the shadow of a set of steps, steps leading up to a shop doorway – 'here!'

They looked up at the sign, high above the door. It said:

Clabbity's Clockwork Curiosities, Puppetry & Toys.

'The toy shop!' gasped Gobkin. 'This is the best detour *ever*!'

The room in the hotel was just like any other room in any other hotel. It had a double bed with a hard mattress and far too many cushions. A rail to hang clothes but with only one crooked wire coat hanger. A little bathroom with tiny beige bottles of shampoo and shower gel. A *DO NOT DISTURB* sign hanging from the outside door handle. But this hotel room had one extra item that would not feature in any brochure or review: a chalk circle drawn on the carpet, in which burned a mysterious purple fire. This last item was Claudia Slymark's contribution.

The three ghost bottles stood on a table, next to the room service menu, so that the seekers could have a good view of the proceedings.

'I believe the otherworldly inferno is nearly ready, Miss Slymark,' said Totherbligh, observing the flames. There was no heat generated – in fact the fire burned cold, turning from purple to a frosted blue. 'Are you prepared to perform the enchantment?'

Claudia cast a glance over the spell book. She was not a witch – there were schools for people who wanted to learn that kind of thing, and Claudia had never been fond of homework. But that didn't mean she couldn't perform a little bit of magic. Like any job, it was just a matter of having the right tools. In this case, it was a folio of basic enchantments she had stolen from a library in Addis Ababa. The client had haggled over the price, saying it wasn't worth what he'd paid, so she'd kept it for herself. It had helped her out of a few sticky situations, but Claudia preferred to rely on her earthly skills for the most part. Especially when the spell asked for ingredients such as Deadman's Shroud, a plant she had spent half the night scouring for in the local graveyard. Conjuring the fire had taken up all of the morning. This had better work.

'I think all is in order,' she said. She unfolded a map of the town, almost identical to the wallpaper of the Sprouts' kitchen, and laid it on the bed. Then she produced the toothpick from her bag. Hinchsniff's bottle trembled in anticipation. Soon the hunt for the wretched little people would be on again!

Claudia snapped the stick in half and threw it into the fire. The flames shuddered and swallowed up the tiny spear. In order to work, a finding spell needed an object owned by the individual who was to be found.

'*Egovenari!*' Claudia chanted. '*Egovenari! Egovenari!*'

There was a momentary pause. There was always a pause. Part of magic's appeal was the drama, Claudia had decided. Then a blue sphere, the size of a marble, rose from the fire and spun in mid-air. It glowed with a cold, white light. Claudia pointed a long finger at the map (not her own finger but a wand made from the finger bones of an ancient druid that came with the spell book) and the sphere flew straight at it, hitting a spot almost exactly in its centre. It exploded on contact, leaving behind a blue dot on the paper.

'Toads in custard!' exclaimed Peggy Gums.

'Oh, Miss Slymark!' said Totherbligh, his ghostly

12

Into Wonderland

The toy shop door had a letterbox at its base with a conveniently loose spring on the flap, so it was easy for Gafferty and Gobkin to push themselves through and into the shop. For several minutes they just stood on the doormat and stared open-mouthed.

They knew of Clabbity's from tales told by Mum and Dad, and had been promised a trip there when Grub was older. But their parents' stories hadn't quite prepared them for the spectacle that lay before them. It was the Smidgen version of a theme park, a magical wonderland of little people's dreams made real. From the shelves laden with farm animals, construction kits, model robots and dinosaurs to the display cases filled with doll's houses,

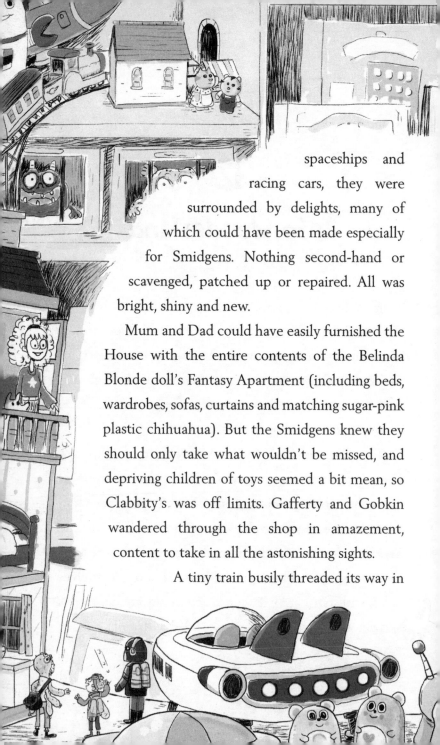

spaceships and racing cars, they were surrounded by delights, many of which could have been made especially for Smidgens. Nothing second-hand or scavenged, patched up or repaired. All was bright, shiny and new.

Mum and Dad could have easily furnished the House with the entire contents of the Belinda Blonde doll's Fantasy Apartment (including beds, wardrobes, sofas, curtains and matching sugar-pink plastic chihuahua). But the Smidgens knew they should only take what wouldn't be missed, and depriving children of toys seemed a bit mean, so Clabbity's was off limits. Gafferty and Gobkin wandered through the shop in amazement, content to take in all the astonishing sights.

A tiny train busily threaded its way in

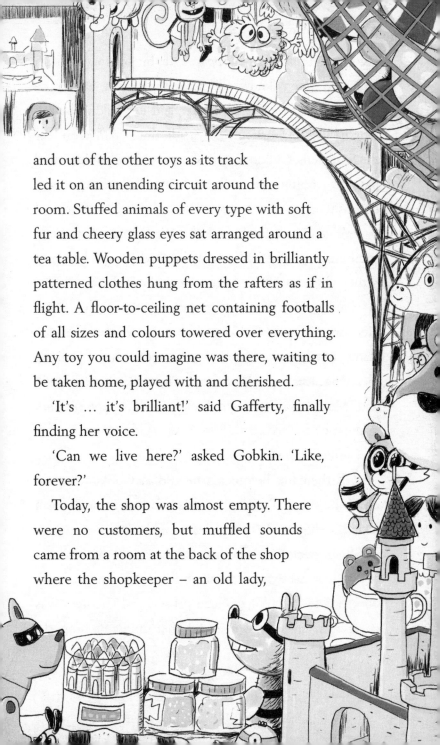

and out of the other toys as its track led it on an unending circuit around the room. Stuffed animals of every type with soft fur and cheery glass eyes sat arranged around a tea table. Wooden puppets dressed in brilliantly patterned clothes hung from the rafters as if in flight. A floor-to-ceiling net containing footballs of all sizes and colours towered over everything. Any toy you could imagine was there, waiting to be taken home, played with and cherished.

'It's … it's brilliant!' said Gafferty, finally finding her voice.

'Can we live here?' asked Gobkin. 'Like, forever?'

Today, the shop was almost empty. There were no customers, but muffled sounds came from a room at the back of the shop where the shopkeeper – an old lady, according to Mum – appeared to be sorting through boxes. Gafferty knew the town's children would be coming out of their school soon, and it wouldn't be too long before they arrived and made things dangerous for the Smidgens. Children were sharp-eyed and, unlike their parents, wouldn't be easily fooled by the creepy-crawly disguises.

'We can't stay long,' she said. 'And we don't want to spoil our trip here with Mum and Dad. They'll be upset if they work out we've been here without them.'

'Can't we at least have a go on Action Dan's Turbo Helicopter?' said Gobkin, running towards a display stand filled with action figure accessories. 'I've no idea what it is but the box says it's got Battle Sound FX and Maximum Karnage Rockets, which sound very impressive!'

Gafferty rolled her eyes.

'OK then, but be quick,' she said, as Gobkin climbed on to the stand. 'I'll keep searching for the moot. It can't be in the shop itself. There must be a cellar or something.'

She inspected the floor around them, seeking evidence of Smidgen activity – mouseholes, cracks in the wall, doors made to look like electrical sockets. The floor was covered in an old worn carpet that didn't fit properly, leaving a gap against one wall and exposing the wooden floorboards. There wasn't enough of a space between the boards for Gafferty to squeeze through, but she could at least have a peek and find out if there was anything worth exploring below.

She knelt by the skirting board and peered into the darkness under the floor. It was no good – she'd need a light to see anything down there. *If* there was anything. She was beginning to doubt if this was the right location after all. A toy shop did seem a bit unlikely.

As she got to her feet, her eye was drawn to some scratches in the skirting board – not scratches, she realised, but a carving. Far too small for Big Folk to notice. A triangle, a circle and another upside-down triangle. The symbols from the book, the symbols Gafferty had guessed represented the three clans! Smidgens had been here before.

Did the presence of all three symbols mean that all three clans had been here together, meeting up for the Smidgenmoot? Her hopes began to rise. Still, there was no clue to where the Smidgenmoot might be. She looked closer at the carving. The circle was more strongly outlined, the shape scored deeply into the wood. It was a button. She reached out to press it then quickly withdrew her hand as the shop bell clattered noisily. The door opened. Customers!

Please let Gobkin remember Rule One of the Smidgens, thought Gafferty as she threw herself behind a huge teddy bear that sat on the floor. *Stay hidden and observe.* She risked a glance, silently parting the toy's thick fur like a hunter might stalk their prey through long grass.

The customer was an unlikely toy buyer. A tall woman elegantly dressed in a long coat and wearing sunglasses. An unusual necklace of coloured glass beads rattled as she stepped into the shop. Gafferty watched as the customer scanned the room, her dark glasses mirroring the colourful objects on display. She was looking for something, but Gafferty wasn't sure it was a new toy she was after. There was a malevolent air to this lady. She loomed over the model of a castle, overshadowing its defenceless toy soldiers, like a giantess from a fairytale.

'They must be here,' she said, as if talking to an invisible companion. She lowered her glasses and her eyes darted back and forth from shelf to shelf. 'The spell worked, didn't it?'

Gafferty gripped the teddy tightly. The spell? Who *was* this lady? And who was she talking to? Then, to Gafferty's horror, the woman moved towards the display of action figures, towards the helicopter her brother was so keen to try out.

'They're close,' she said. 'I know it! The Smidgens are here somewhere! And if they're here, perhaps the Mirror of Trokanis is nearby too.'

'She's some kind of witch!' Gafferty gasped. 'And she's hunting for us – oh no, Gobkin! What have I done?'

Her brother was in trouble and it was all her fault.

13

Claudia Goes Shopping

'Can I help you?' A smiling, round, wrinkled face appeared from behind the counter.

Claudia glared at the old woman for daring to interrupt her business.

'I'm ... just browsing, thank you,' she said awkwardly. She was used to doing reconnaissance missions before a job, pretending to be a tourist or a traffic warden, or something like that. But usually in banks and museums, not toy shops. Hopefully, the old biddy would go away. There was a stifled sniggering from the bottles at her neck.

'I see you're admiring our action figure range,' the shopkeeper said, deliberately ignoring the hint. She sensed wealth in the customer's clothing and demeanour. There could be a sale here. She pointed to a shelf of figures with plastic wings and armour, and Viking-style helmets with large round eyes stuck to them. 'The Bug Knights are extremely popular at the moment. They're characters from a cartoon series, you know. Little insect people. Lots of different ones to collect. Children do so like to collect things, don't they?'

Claudia forced a smile at the shopkeeper. Why was the old fool still speaking … ?

'Wait – did you say *insect* people?'

She turned to the display of Bug Knights. The Smidgens at the burger bar had been dressed as insects. Could they be hiding amongst the toys, trying to blend in? The

shopkeeper wasn't wrong: there were loads of the characters, all lined up in rows on the shelf. Claudia's gaze swept across them, watching for any movement, a breath, a blink of an eye. She sniffed suspiciously. There was a fly boy in the back row, he looked a bit paler than the others, his costume a little scruffier. Did he just wriggle his nose? Could he—?

She jumped as an explosion of children crashed through the door and swarmed about the shop, talking, laughing and screaming in an untidy river of noise. Before she could act, they shoved their way around Claudia, knocking her sunglasses askew, jostling her from all sides and carrying her far from the action figures on a current of elbows. She tried to wade back through, but it was impossible – the children had numbers on their side. The pack leader, a girl with a mess of brown hair and a mouth as wide as a sinkhole, pushed through the crowd and made straight for the counter, bellowing a greeting to the shopkeeper.

'Oh my god Miss Clabbity how are you oh my god what a day I thought I'd never get here it's my birthday next week I'm eleven and I'm having a party so I need balloons loads of them and do you have that game with the thing it's really funny I've seen it on the TV you have to crawl on all fours I bet I'd be good at it but oh my god I bet if Vanessa had to crawl around she'd do a gigantic fart like she did in gym class today –' there was a pause as everyone burst into laughter at the memory of Vanessa in gym class, except for Vanessa, who blushed – 'and Mr Trap he's our gym teacher he was so cross his face screwed up and went bright purple and it looked exactly like a monkey's bum and oh my god Vanessa did you just let one off again … ?'

Claudia staggered out of the stink and chaos of the shop into the alley, her dignity severely ruffled. She rarely encountered children in her usual line of work and was unfamiliar with their unnerving ability to act like a tornado of clamour, confusion and dirt.

'Savages!' she spat. 'I'm sure I was about to catch one of the Smidgens. I should find a spell in that book to turn all those horrors into worms!'

'Ooh, yes!' said Peggy Gums. 'Worms in a bread roll with beetle chutney. A favourite treat of mine.'

'Perhaps *we* can assist, Miss Slymark?' purred Totherbligh. 'We can be discreet and almost invisible.'

'Yes!' said Hinchsniff, eagerly. 'Let us out!'

'Not you,' said Claudia to Hinchsniff, regaining her composure. 'You had a chance and failed.' She smoothed her hair and unstopped the green bottle. A grey mist poured out into the alley. 'Totherbligh – it's your turn.'

Gafferty leaped out from behind the cover of the teddy bear and ran towards the display of action figures. She had to reach Gobkin and then get them both out of there! The witch-lady had left the shop but there was still the danger from the children. Their heavy feet were stomping all over the floor as they checked out the latest toys and games, and chatted, laughed and argued with each other. Gafferty dived behind a model of a moon rocket just in time to avoid being crushed by a school bag dumped carelessly on the floor. She'd have to be quick and vigilant if they were to leave the shop in one piece.

She spied Gobkin high up on the Bug Knights display. He must have climbed up there to hide when the woman came in. Thank goodness he was all right! He saw her and waved. He was pointing to something – the train track. What was he trying to tell her? Gafferty had never seen a real train but Gobkin had read about it in the *Big Book* so she knew that it was another machine the Big Folk used to move themselves about. It must be quite difficult carrying all that flesh and hair around all the time, she supposed.

She followed the track with her eyes. It wound through the shop in a gentle spiral, taking the train not only around and around but up and down as well, supported on specially made bridges and viaducts, passing the shelf where Gobkin was hiding. Gob was going to catch the train to get back to floor level! If he crouched down, he would fit neatly into the open carriage that the engine towed behind it. He was using Rule Four of the Smidgens: *if in doubt, make it up!* Gafferty signalled a thumbs up, though her heart beat faster at the thought. Her little brother was up there all on his own, taking risks when she should be looking after him. Mum and Dad would be furious with her if they knew!

She watched as the little train slowly made its way up to Gobkin's shelf, the highest point on its journey. Without anyone noticing, he tumbled into the carriage and the train continued onwards, picking up speed as it began its downward journey.

'Miss Clabbity!' a boy shouted above the sounds of his friends. 'Did you turn the heating off? It's freezing in here.'

He was right. Gafferty noticed the cold too. A familiar kind of cold. The hairs on the back of her neck rose as she saw a pale shape sliding through the letterbox, just as she and Gobkin had done earlier. It slithered around the toys, keeping out of sight of the children, hiding its creeping, menacing form. Gafferty let out a quiet cry of fear. It was the thing from the tunnel, or something very much like it! She remembered the creature had mentioned a 'she' – *What does she want with you? What does she want with something so small?* it had said. 'She' must be that woman! The creatures and the woman were working together to find and catch Smidgens. But why?

There wasn't time to think any more about it – the monster snaked along the railway, moving with purpose. Gafferty froze, filled with dread. It had spotted Gobkin and was making straight for him!

14

The Smidgen Express

She watched helplessly as the creature advanced. How could she alert Gobkin to the danger? She couldn't yell a warning to him – it might attract the attention of the human children! And besides, what could he possibly do whilst trapped on a moving train? It was racing along at speed now, and she could see Gob enjoying the ride, hanging on to the carriage tightly and unaware of the threat heading straight for him.

Gafferty shook herself out of her daze – she had to do something!

'Rule Four,' she said to herself, looking around in panic for ideas. 'Rule Four, Rule Four don't let me down … aha!'

The moon rocket stood next to the Belinda Blonde doll shelf. Belinda and all her various outfits and accessories were on show, a wall of frills and so much pink it gave Gafferty a headache. Thankfully, Belinda was quite sporty. There was a skateboard (pink) and an ice hockey stick (also pink). Belinda was four times the size of Gafferty, so the skateboard and hockey stick were huge, but they were made from thin plastic and just about light enough to carry.

Gafferty dragged them to the nearest bit of railway track. She was in luck: the skateboard wheels slotted neatly on to the metal rails. Despite the grim situation, she laughed.

'I've got my own train!' she said. 'Thanks, Belinda!'

She climbed on to the board and used the hockey stick to propel herself forward like a gondolier rowing a boat along a canal. It was hard work, but the first section of the track was flat so, once she had got going, she began to build up speed. Soon she was whipping around the twists of the railway on her way to rescue her brother. Hopefully, the children in the shop were so used to seeing the old train they wouldn't notice the unusual new pink addition surfing along the track as well.

As she swept around a bend, Gafferty kept an eye on

the shapeless smoke-creature stalking Gobkin, her stomach knotted with anxiety. It moved like a hunting cat, smoothly gliding from one place of cover to another, carefully choosing its moment to slip closer and closer towards the unsuspecting boy in his tiny train. It paused for a second, as still as the lifeless toys around it. Then Gafferty saw the monster suddenly crouch, ready to pounce. A hand launched out to snatch Gobkin from his carriage.

'Gobkin!' she squealed, as loudly as she dared. 'Look out!' Then, just at the last minute, the train sped into a tunnel of display cases, carrying Gobkin out of sight and out of the creature's clutches. Seconds later the train reappeared on the other side of the shop with the boy safe and sound and still having no idea about his near miss.

'Oh, Gobkin!' Gafferty sighed with relief. His good fortune had held but it wouldn't be long before the thing caught up with him.

She hadn't given much thought to what she was going to do, but Gafferty knew she wasn't going to let the monster have her brother, even if it meant offering herself in his place. If the woman wanted a Smidgen, she could have one, but Gafferty was going to make sure she regretted it. Her free hand reached into her bag. It immediately found the knife, its smooth surface quivering strangely at her touch. Gafferty dearly hoped she wouldn't have to use it, but she drew the weapon out and clasped it tightly.

She was travelling in the opposite direction to Gobkin and they were rapidly coming to a point on the track where they would meet. Where they would meet … oh no! She had a horrible realisation: there was no way of stopping either the train or the skateboard – they were going to collide!

'So much for making it up!' Gafferty muttered, furious at her stupidity. 'I'll never bother with Rule Four again!'

It was then that Gobkin spotted her on the track in front of him. He grinned in surprise, but his smile was replaced by a look of alarm as they hurtled towards each other. Closer and closer. Faster and faster.

'Jump!' Gafferty shouted. 'Gobkin – jump!' She pointed to a pile of soft toys lying by the track. If they timed this right, they'd both land safely amongst the padded, fur-covered animals. Gobkin nodded but Gafferty could see him biting his lip anxiously. He was losing his nerve. He was too scared, the distance was too great, he wouldn't be able to do it! 'Gob!' she screamed. 'Jump NOW!'

Everything happened at once and yet, to Gafferty, time seemed to slow down. She watched Gobkin hurl himself from the carriage, his arms and legs flailing. Seeing him clear the track, she dived into the toys, just as the train ploughed into the skateboard. The pink board flipped up into the air, somersaulting over the engine, which bucked and bounced off the rails. Then, to her dismay, a grey hand billowed out of nowhere, swooping toward them, its cold fingers grasping for Gobkin and plucking him out of mid-air.

'Gobkin!' Gafferty shrieked as she collided with the pile of toys. She scrambled to her feet and leaped at the hand that was carrying her astonished brother out of reach, back towards the door. She swung the knife, uselessly – she was too far away to do any damage. But static suddenly crackled through the air, streaming out from the glass blade, which glowed with a soft rose-coloured light. It struck the hand and the creature yelped in pain. It recoiled like a surprised serpent. Gafferty was as taken aback as the monster. Where had that energy come from?

'Gafferty!' Gobkin cried. 'What's going on? Help me!'

There wasn't time to ask questions – the thing had stubbornly held on to her brother. He floated above the ground as the misty hand bore him across the shop. She clambered out of the pile of toys to give chase.

'Miss Clabbity, your train's crashed!' one of the children shouted. 'I saw sparks, too.'

Someone would be coming to investigate. That was all she needed. But Gafferty didn't care if the Big Folk saw her – her little brother had been kidnapped by the witch and her monsters and she was going to get him back! She sprinted towards the door, but it was already too late: she heard the letterbox slam shut behind Gobkin as he was carried off into the street.

'No!' she wanted to shout, but a hand, this time fleshy and warm, appeared from behind her and covered her mouth. She was dragged roughly back into the gloom behind a model dinosaur, its vicious teeth casting spiked shadows across the floor.

'Hush!' said a voice behind her ear. 'The Big Folk are right above us! Do you want them to see you?'

The shape of a child passed overhead, paused, and was gone.

Gafferty pulled away from the stranger's grip and turned on them ferociously.

'Take your hands off me!' she began, waving the knife haphazardly. 'My brother's just been taken by a witch and if you think …' and then she stopped.

She was face-to-face with a boy. A boy her own size, her own age.

'You're …' she began, not quite believing what she saw in front of her. 'You're like me. You're a *Smidgen*!'

15

Willoughby

It was what she had dreamed of for so long: meeting another of her own kind. Yet so many emotions boiled in Gafferty's head – fear, guilt, worry, surprise, curiosity, excitement – they ended up crowding each other out, leaving her numb and suddenly drained.

She stared at the boy, bewildered. He wore a rucksack over a jacket with tails, and buckled to his head was a crash helmet that had large eyes and a beak drawn on it. He was dressed as a bird, perhaps a sparrow, albeit one without any wings. He backed away from her, his eyes on the knife. She quickly put it back in her bag.

'Of course I'm a Smidgen,' he said, scowling. 'What are you doing here? You know this place is out of bounds.

And yes, I know that means I shouldn't be here either, but never mind that …' Then he looked at her more closely. 'I don't think I've seen you at the Roost. Who *are* you?'

'I'm not from the … the Roost,' she said weakly. 'I'm Gafferty Sprout. And I came here searching for other Smidgens because, well, because I don't know any apart from my family. I think I'm from a different clan to you. And I brought my little brother with me and—'

'An outsider!' There was a look of panic on the boy's

face. 'Oh no – I'm really in trouble now!' He peeked out at the shop floor. There was still plenty of noise, but the children were starting to leave. 'The coast is clear. I'd better be going.'

'Wait!' she said, and all the emotions came flooding back. The image of Gobkin's frightened face filled her head. Her voice became scratchy, tears stung her eyes. 'My brother's been kidnapped by a woman – a witch maybe – and she has horrible monsters helping her, and I don't know what to do. It would be really good to have someone to talk to right now.' She sank to the ground and buried her face in her hands, trying not to sob. She'd lost Gobkin when she was meant to be looking after him. How could she ever go home again? How could she explain this to Mum and Dad?

The boy hesitated.

'I'm sorry,' he said, waving his hands about awkwardly, 'but I'd be no help – honest. I'm so useless at everything, always getting things wrong, always making mistakes, and always getting shouted at for it. I broke my wings, so I'll get shouted at for that, and came to the shop – where I'm not supposed to be – to try and pinch one of the toy gliders to replace them, so that'll be another shouting. And I don't want to make things worse by talking to an outsider. I don't know if that's allowed, you see.'

'I'll give you a shouting if you don't shut up, you woolly worry-worm!' said Gafferty, with a sniff. This wasn't at all how she'd imagined her first meeting with another Smidgen. What did this strange boy mean about 'wings'? She looked up at him. 'Please, I need help. I can't face my parents until I get my brother back. Don't you have family? What would you do?'

The boy studied her, thoughtfully. He had a kind face with large, anxious brown eyes and a mouth that obviously smiled a lot, when he wasn't in trouble.

'Maybe my Uncle Abel can help,' he said finally. 'Or he'll know someone who'll know what to do.' He offered her his hand. She smiled gratefully and took it, and he pulled her to her feet. 'My name's Willoughby Woblyn. Come on, we'd better get moving.'

He led her across the shop, a convoluted path from one hiding place to another.

'Why are we going this way?' Gafferty asked, tugging his arm urgently. 'We should go into the street and follow the witch – we should be chasing them!'

'There'll be plenty of eyes watching them,' Willoughby said. 'Don't worry, we'll find them, I'm sure. This is the way home.'

They arrived at the skirting board where Gafferty had discovered the symbols. Willoughby pressed the circular mark in the carving. It was a button, just as Gafferty had guessed! There was a quiet click from behind the board and it slid a few centimetres to one side, leaving a gap exactly the right size for a Smidgen to pass through. Behind it, a set of tiny steps led down into the ground.

'I don't have a torch,' Willoughby said sheepishly as they descended. 'I dropped it and it broke. So be careful.' The board closed behind them, sinking the stairway into darkness. Gafferty kept a hand on the wall as she followed the boy and scolded herself for letting Gobkin carry all the match-heads in his bag.

'It's getting lighter,' she said after a few steps. 'I thought you didn't have a torch.'

He turned mid-step.

'No. It's you,' he said. 'Look.'

He pointed at the scavenger bag, slung on Gafferty's shoulder. Sure enough, it was gleaming with a soft, pinkish radiance. Gafferty opened it and peered inside.

'My knife. My glass knife … it's shining! Like when that weird thing happened with the monster.'

She carefully drew it out, holding it up so that it lit up

the tunnel with its rosy glow. Everything beyond was suddenly visible.

'Why is it doing that?' Willoughby asked.

'I don't know,' she said, absently. She was more interested in what the strange light revealed.

They were standing at the top of a rockface. A huge circular cavern lay below, its high walls covered in animal-shaped carvings. At its centre was a platform, a slab of smooth, dark rock. Surrounding this were many tiers of Smidgen-sized seats. It was like a vast stadium or theatre. Despite the knife only providing a gentle light, somehow it managed to illuminate the entire chamber.

'This is it!' Gafferty said. 'I was right. The Smidgen-moot! Where all the Smidgens come together.' Her voice echoed across the empty cave. 'It's awesome!'

Willoughby frowned.

'Not any more,' he said. 'It's another forbidden place. A ruin. I think it's creepy. But it's the only way to get to the shop from the Roost if you don't have any wings. My brother showed it to me once. Let's get to the other side quickly.'

They scrambled down more steps that hugged the cavern wall. Gafferty was disappointed not to see the moot filled with people. It couldn't have been used for many years. But her disappointment was lessened by the incredible atmosphere of the cave – her own people had created this, something so magnificent! It wasn't creepy at all. As they reached the platform at the centre of the amphitheatre, encircled by layer upon layer of seating, she imagined the huge audience that might assemble there, imagined them all cheering for her and leaning in to catch every word she said. She felt her heart lift towards the ceiling far above and fill with hope.

'Gob, I'm coming to get you, I promise,' she said under her breath. 'I'll get you as much strawberry jam as you can eat when this is all over. Just hold on – I'm on my way …'

16

The Voice in the Glass

The knife shone more brightly as they approached the platform. Gafferty stepped on to the black table of rock, the pink glow reflected in its polished surface. She noticed it wasn't entirely flat. There was a pile of rubble at one end. A stone structure of some kind had either been broken or collapsed there. Perhaps it had been a statue.

'Your knife is putting on quite a show,' observed Willoughby. Spots of light emerged from the blade and orbited Gafferty's hand, as if the knife were on fire, but Gafferty felt no heat. Just an odd tingling sensation that ran through her.

'It has a connection to this place,' she said. She held the weapon up like a torch. 'I feel like it's trying to tell me something. I'm sure it was trying to protect Gobkin and me from the monster. I thought it had a personality the first time I touched it. But there's more to it than that. There's some power in it.'

As she spoke, she heard words that were not her own. There was another voice: she knew it was coming from the knife and yet the sounds echoed inside her head. The words didn't make any sense. It was as if she were listening to fragments of a conversation broken into pieces.

'Can you hear that?' she said.

'What?' Willoughby stared at her.

'That … that sound. A voice. It's faded now. I think it was from the knife. Couldn't you hear it?'

'I didn't hear anything.' Willoughby's eyes narrowed. *He thinks I'm mad,* Gafferty thought.

The knife-light suddenly changed colour, switching to dark purple. It cast deep shadows throughout the cavern, black, gaunt shapes creeping and skulking across the walls, cavorting in the silence. Gafferty was aware she could hear herself breathing – short, nervous gasps – and felt a chill run down her spine, as if her bones were being prodded by spikes of ice. It was too silent. Was there someone there? Had the smoke monsters followed them?

She spun around, scanning the chamber, but the rapid movement of the knife only made the shadows dance faster, the silhouettes rising and falling in a frenzy. Animal shapes, savage creatures with many limbs and snarling mouths, all twirling and swaying together. Dragons danced with serpents, wolves with giants.

'Stop!' Willoughby's hand grabbed her wrist, halting her mid-spin. The dancers paused, their soundless music ended. 'What are you doing?' His voice was shaky. She was scaring him.

'I thought there was something there,' she whispered. 'I felt like I was being watched.'

Willoughby stepped away from the platform. He looked around nervously.

'I don't see anything.'

He was right. There was nothing to see. Only shadows.

'Come on,' he said. 'Let's go.'

Gafferty reluctantly turned to follow him but her eye caught a twitch of movement. One shadow had stirred. By itself.

She turned back, missed her footing in her haste and fell from the platform straight into the back of Willoughby.

'Watch out!' he said, elbowing her away.

'I saw something move! At least, I think I did.' They both glanced behind them. Everything was still.

'There's *nothing* there.' Willoughby was cross now. 'We haven't got time for this weirdness. I thought you wanted help.'

Yes, Gobkin, Gafferty thought. He was all that mattered now. She needed to focus. She didn't have time for magical talking cutlery and imaginary shadow things. She nodded guiltily.

They hurried from the chamber, Gafferty risking a last look behind her. Whatever she had seen, or thought she had seen, it was gone, although the fear, the sense of being watched, didn't leave her until they had passed through an archway at the chamber's edge. As she tucked the knife in her belt, its colour returned to pink, the light dimming with every step.

They walked in silence for a few minutes before her curiosity got the better of her.

'The symbols on the skirting board,' she asked, as they followed another tunnel. 'Do you know what they mean?'

'Not really,' Willoughby said grumpily. 'Though I've seen the second triangle in several places at the Roost.'

'I think they stand for the three clans of Smidgens.' She brought out the atlas and showed him the book's cover. The knife still gave enough light to see the pages. She turned to the page with the Smidgenmoot. 'This book can show me all the routes of the Tangle. See? Here's the tunnel we're walking through.'

'I don't know anything about any clans,' said Willoughby, ignoring the atlas and walking on. 'There's only ever been us in the Roost. We don't use the tunnels much. I know of the Tangle but never been into it beyond this bit. It's not allowed.'

These Smidgens have a lot of things that aren't allowed, thought Gafferty. *That's not how Gafferty Sprout does things.*

'I guess that's why I've never seen any other Smidgens in the Tangle,' she said. 'If you're scared of it.'

'We're not scared.' He shot her a look. He was annoyed but still uneasy. 'It's being sensible. It's dangerous in here. We're near the very centre of it, the darkest part. Don't you know there are bad things hiding in there? You must have heard the stories. And anyway, we have a better way of getting about.'

'Your so-called wings? You don't really fly, do you?'

Gafferty couldn't quite believe it. Smidgens belonged underground, not up in the air with the birds.

'You're very argumentative for someone who wants to make new friends,' Willoughby remarked drily.

Gafferty bit her lip. She wasn't used to talking to people outside her family. She could say what she felt to the other Sprouts and knew they would give as good as they got. But it wasn't going to work with everyone.

'Sorry,' she said. 'I'm only interested. It's so strange to think of other Smidgens out there, other Smidgens doing things differently to the way I've always been taught.'

'It's fine,' he said, although he still sounded irritable. 'I'm sure your own way of doing things works for wherever it is you live.'

'In the House – here.' She turned to the page in the atlas showing her home. 'See, it has the other triangle symbol.' Then she flicked back to the page showing the tower with the upside-down triangle next to it. 'Is that where we're going?' she asked, showing it to the boy.

'Yes – that's the Roost. Maybe you're right about the symbols.'

'I don't remember ever seeing a building like this in the town, or at least in the parts I visited with my mum and dad.'

He smiled. It was the first time she'd seen him smile. It suited him.

'It looks different now,' he said. 'You'll see.'

The tunnel had climbed back up to street level, as Gafferty soon discovered. It ended in a doorway that opened into a shallow drain, running under the surface of the road. They clambered out of the drain grille and into the street, busy with people coming out of work. They would have to keep their wits about them, as there were lots of quick, trampling feet to avoid. But on the upside, no one was paying attention to anything other than getting home. The two Smidgens dashed across the pavement and stopped behind a rubbish bin.

'I've not been here before,' Gafferty said. 'Do we have to go much further?'

'Nope – this is it,' said Willoughby. 'This is where we live.'

The building that stood before them was many storeys high and ran the length of the street. Everything about it was meant to impress. From the engraved stone columns on either side of the wide doors, to the large windows framed by rich velvet curtains, to the huge, illuminated sign that hung over them.

'*Hotel*,' Gafferty read. 'You live here? It's the biggest

Big Folk building I've ever seen! What do the Big Folk do in it?'

'They sleep and eat in it. It's a place for Big Folk from other towns to stay in when they visit this town.'

Gafferty gaped at him.

'There are *other* towns? Other Big Folk towns?'

He grinned.

'Didn't you know? There are lots of other towns. Hundreds probably. And lots and lots of other Big Folk.'

Gafferty put her hand against the bin to steady herself. It had never occurred to her that there might be places outside the town she knew – it was so enormous already! *The Big Book of Big Folk Facts* had never said anything about this! Did Mum and Dad know? Did those towns have Smidgens too? There wasn't time to take it all in. She'd have to think about this revelation later. Willoughby was pointing to the far end of the hotel.

'We only live in that one bit of it. Down there.'

The hotel was old and grand but Gafferty realised the structure attached to its end was much older, with a wall built from large, irregular stones. This circular wall had a conical roof at its top with one large window. It was like a very ancient stone rocket had been stuck on to the oblong of the main building.

'The tower in the atlas!' Gafferty said.

'That's it. In ancient times the Big Folk used it as a lookout tower, to protect the town from marauding invaders – from *other* towns. Now it's just a stairwell, a fire exit. The Roost is hidden inside.'

'So, you fly there. On your wings.'

He laughed.

'Normally. But as I don't have any wings, I'm afraid we're going to have to go in by the front door.'

17

Claudia Versus Gobkin

Gobkin opened his eyes. He felt cold and drowsy. What had happened? Where was he?

He tried to focus. He was lying on a table in a human bedroom. There was a tall folded piece of card standing on the table next to him with the words *hotel* and *menu* written on it. It had a list of sandwiches which sounded very tasty. His tummy rumbled.

'Have I been asleep?' he said aloud, though he wasn't sure who he was asking.

'In a manner of speaking.' The voice came from near a window. Gobkin remembered: the tall woman with the cruel smile! He'd been snatched by that thing in the toy shop. It had carried him out to the woman, who'd been waiting in the street outside. Her face reminded him of a cat he had once seen eyeing up a mouse for dinner. Then everything had gone dark.

'What did you do to me?' he demanded. He sat up and looked around.

'I didn't do anything.' The woman sat down on the bed opposite him, smiling. 'But my seeker, dear Totherbligh, froze you – it's called ghost-paralysis, or fright-freeze – to keep you quiet and still. It took a couple of attempts, mind you. You're certainly tougher than anyone might expect.'

'Ghost-paralysis.' He stared at the woman. She seemed very much alive. 'You're not a ghost.'

'I'm not. But *they* are.'

The air moved in front of him and began to take shape. Three figures appeared on the bed around her: a shifty brute of a man who stared at him hungrily from under wolfish eyebrows, a blubbery man who resembled a bad-tempered walrus, and a kindly old lady who appeared to be knitting with ghostly wool. She smiled at him, revealing fangs sharp and pointed like a shark's.

'My seekers,' said the woman, gazing fondly at her companions. 'As the day's light fades, they become more visible.'

Gobkin shivered. He remembered the cold touch of the hand that caught him. He'd never seen a ghost before, never mind three sitting together. He felt scared and alone and very, very small. But he was hungry and angry and not in the mood for Big Folk and their nonsense. He'd always thought humans were silly and this was more proof, as far as he was concerned.

'If you're not a ghost then you must be a witch,' he said.

The woman shook her head and leaned towards him.

'My name is Claudia Slymark,' she said. 'I am what is known as an acquisitions agent.'

'I'm Gobkin Sprout and I am what is known as *annoyed*. I want to go home and have my dinner.' He folded his arms and scowled. 'What's an acquisitions agent anyway?'

'I am hired by clients who wish to purchase objects that are … difficult to obtain by normal means. Objects of high value.'

'You're a thief,' said Gobkin. 'A thief who's friendly with ghosts. Though I don't know why you'd want to bother with dead people. The living ones are enough trouble.'

The ghosts chuckled. Claudia raised an eyebrow.

'You are here,' she said, firmly, 'so I can learn about

you. And your family. I would like to meet them. I would like to know all about them.'

'Why? I'm not stupid. Everyone knows thieves are the bad guys. Except for Smidgens, of course – we only take what no one will miss. And you don't hang out with spooks unless you're up to no good. What are you really after?'

Claudia smiled.

'You're very amusing. But you're quite right. I am after something. Perhaps you can help me? A magical item – the Mirror of Trokanis, it's called. I have a client who is very interested in its whereabouts. Do you know anything about it, young Gobkin?'

Gobkin had never heard of any Mirror, but then he was always the last to be told about important stuff. It would be typical of Mum and Dad to keep something interesting from him. *I bet Gafferty knows about it*, he thought. It made him more annoyed.

'Maybe I do know,' he said sulkily. 'And maybe I don't. Either way, I'm not saying a word until I've had my dinner.'

Claudia sighed.

'Very well,' she said. 'I'm not unreasonable. I can wait a while. And I'm quite hungry myself. I will bring you some food back from dinner and then we will talk. But you'd better have some answers for me, boy. I would hate to have to ask my friends here to force them out of you.'

The first challenge Gafferty and Willoughby faced was how to get through the hotel entrance. There was a lot of bustle and activity as guests arrived to check into their rooms for the night. Then there was the door itself.

'It revolves,' said Willoughby as, from their hiding place behind a potted palm tree that decorated the building's exterior, they watched a woman jump out of a taxi that drew up at the hotel steps. She pushed awkwardly through the entrance, the intersecting doors spinning around like a propeller and regurgitating a second guest into the street. 'You have to time it right or you'll get sliced in half!'

'I don't need the gory details,' said Gafferty. 'This needs thought. Me and Dad deal with this stuff every day. You would too if you spent more time on the ground and less time flapping about in the air.'

'Go on, then,' said Willoughby, shoving her forward. 'Show me how it's done, Miss Expert.'

Gafferty didn't really have a clue what she was going

to do – she'd only been out in the Big World a few times with Dad – but tried to look confident. She needed a bit of luck, that was all. At that moment, a man with a bag and umbrella trotted up the steps from the street. The umbrella was a tall, old-fashioned type with a heavy cane handle and was partly open, the folds of fabric gently flapping as its owner walked.

'That's my bit of luck,' said Gafferty. She beckoned to Willoughby and they raced towards the human. Undoing her bag, she brought out a pin hook, one end of which was tied to the rope of fishing line. When she was dangerously close to the man's feet, Gafferty twirled the hook over her head then released it, sending it like a dart into a fold of the umbrella. She tugged the other end of the rope – it was secure. As the man stepped forward, he dragged Gafferty with him, lifting her feet off the ground.

'Grab my hand!' she called. Willoughby only just managed to reach her before they were both flung into the material of the umbrella. They hung on tightly as the man pushed through the door, Willoughby grinning with excitement. He'd clearly never had a lift from a human! *Dad would be so mad at me for taking this kind of risk*, thought Gafferty. *But sometimes Rule Four raises its ugly head and there's nothing you can do but obey it!*

As soon as they were safely in the lobby, Gafferty unhooked the line. They slid down the umbrella fold and dropped to the floor, immediately running to safety under a nearby sofa.

'We made it!' said Willoughby, catching his breath. 'That was amazing! Gafferty? Are you OK?'

Gafferty was staring up the lobby stairs, her mouth open in horror. There was a woman walking down towards them.

'It's *her*!' she hissed. 'She's here. The woman who snatched Gobkin is in the hotel!'

18

Dinner for Four

Claudia swept into the hotel restaurant. A young, keen waiter tried to guide her to a table for one in a badly lit corner, but she brushed past him and seated herself at a larger, roomier table near the window. With a look that could freeze concrete, Claudia sent the waiter scurrying away.

'You're being very tolerant of the young Smidgen, Miss Slymark,' said Totherbligh, now back in his bottle. 'He was very rude to you.'

'Yes,' muttered Hinchsniff, from the neighbouring bottle. 'We should have squeezed him like a grape until he screamed for mercy.'

'A glass of Smidgen-juice,' agreed Peggy Gums. 'With a little umbrella in it.'

'I'm not a fan of violence,' Claudia said, reading the dinner menu. 'At least not yet. Little Gobkin Sprout is all I've got, so far. I don't want to damage him.'

'And might we enquire what the Mirror does, Miss Slymark?' said Totherbligh. 'You've never really told us.'

Claudia had deliberately kept the ghosts in the dark during her dealings with her mysterious client. When she had responded to the original letter she had pressed for more details, particularly about her fee. If the client was only offering her vague promises, she wanted to know what the Mirror was worth. If they couldn't be trusted, she might need to hold it back, like the spell book, or find a different buyer.

YOU WILL KNOW THE MIRROR BY ITS RADIANCE, the client had replied in their odd way. A CRYSTAL THE SIZE OF A HUMAN HAND AND THE COLOUR OF THE DAWN SKY. FILLED WITH LIFE FORCE. IT CAN TRANSPORT YOU ANYWHERE YOU WISH JUST BY A THOUGHT. THERE ARE THREE PIECES TO FIND. FIND OUT WHAT THE SMIDGENS KNOW.

Claudia had been even more intrigued. A way of entering any place she chose, any room, anywhere in the world? Locked doors would no longer be a problem.

If this were genuine, the Mirror could potentially offer her a more useful alternative to her ghosts. And she wouldn't have to put up with their quirks, their moods, their unreliability. In short, she could do without them. She decided it was best to keep this information to herself. She was confident she had her seekers under her control but didn't see any reason to put that control to the test.

'I'm not even sure myself what it does,' she said dismissively, arranging her napkin on her lap. 'You know I'm not interested in magic.'

'Yes, Miss Slymark,' Totherbligh said. If he had any other thoughts, he kept them to himself.

'That's her!' said Gafferty from underneath the dessert trolley. She and Willoughby had followed Claudia into the restaurant. 'Didn't you see her come into the toy shop?'

'I only turned up at the shop a few minutes before I met you,' said Willoughby. 'You're sure she's a witch? Do witches stay in hotels?'

'How would I know? If what you said is true, she's not from here. She must be from … some other town. But don't you see? If she's in the hotel, that means Gobkin is too.'

'Not if she's eaten him – that's what Big Folk do when they catch Smidgens. Ouch! That hurt!'

'Say that again and broken wings will be the least of your worries. And anyway, she's having dinner so she can't have eaten already.'

'If your brother isn't with her, he must be in her room. We need to find out her room number.'

'Yes! We can rescue Gobkin whilst she's having dinner and be gone before she knows it.' Gafferty was trying to keep confident but it was getting harder. What did she think she was doing? She was lurching from one disaster to another! This vast, bustling restaurant was as alien a landscape to her as the moon, with its pristine table linen, gilded furniture and prim waiters rushing around doing goodness knows what. Why were the Big Folk making such a huge fuss over a silly meal? She realised she understood almost nothing about the world she lived in. Even clumsy Willoughby knew more than she did.

'The waiter makes a note of the room number when a guest sits down at a table,' he was saying, 'so they know which room to send the dinner bill to. Look – there's the list, on that table next to us.'

Gafferty could just see the piece of paper sticking out

from a clipboard sitting on top of a table high over their heads.

'If you keep watch, I can climb up the tablecloth and have a peek,' she said.

'Don't be daft! It's far too risky!'

'I can do it. I *can*.' Gafferty felt sick with fear, but what choice was there?

They ran from the dessert trolley to the table. The tablecloth covered it right down to the floor, so it was quite easy for Gafferty to pull herself up the starched pleats using a pair of pin hooks, though her arms ached by the time she reached the top and she was painfully aware that her grey spider suit must stick out like a sore thumb against the pure white cloth. She peeped over the edge of the table to see if anyone was looking. Fortunately, the waiters were busy attending to diners, so she dragged herself up and scurried across to the clipboard. On the paper was a map of dinner tables with numbers on them, then a list of the table numbers with a room number beside each one.

'Window table,' Gafferty said to herself as she walked down the list, 'which means she's in room number—'

'SPIDER!'

Gafferty was almost deafened by the scream. There was a lady standing over her, eyes filled with revulsion and a sharp claw of a finger pointing straight at her.

'SPIDER! HUGE, HORRIBLE THING. IT'S PROBABLY POISONOUS. SOMEBODY DO SOME-THING!'

By now, the whole restaurant was staring. Some diners had frozen with horror, spoons and forks halfway to their open mouths. Gafferty couldn't hang about. There was only one thing for it: she sprang to the edge of the table and slid down the cloth as quickly as she could.

'IT'S JUMPED OFF THE TABLE! IT'S ON THE LOOSE! ALL THOSE LEGS! HOW PERFECTLY GHASTLY!'

Some diners stood up and began scanning the floor nervously. One man looked like he was about to jump on his chair. Others were just enjoying the show.

Gafferty landed with a bump in the thick carpet and rolled sideways, dodging the stomping shoe of a waiter, before diving under the cloth to reunite with Willoughby, who stood quaking next to a table leg.

'You were supposed to keep watch!' she hissed, as he pulled her to her feet. 'We'll get caught, you bumble-bonce!'

'I'm sorry,' wailed Willoughby miserably. 'I didn't see her until it was too late. I told you I'm useless.'

The restaurant was in uproar. The waiter, sweat appearing on his forehead, was trying to soothe the woman, but she wasn't going quietly.

'IT'S POISONOUS, I TELL YOU! IF THERE ARE POISONOUS SPIDERS AT LIBERTY IN THIS ESTABLISHMENT, I WILL BE ALERTING THE MEDIA!'

Suddenly everyone was searching the floor for the infamous spider. The two Smidgens cowered in their hiding place.

'We need a distraction so we can escape!' said Gafferty. 'You're meant to be a bird – can't you flap about or drop worms on them or something?'

Willoughby's face brightened.

'I'll fix it,' he said. 'Birds and worms – that's given me an idea.'

The waiter was standing by the table, trying to persuade the irate woman that there was nothing to fear from spiders, and definitely nothing to alert the media about. Willoughby darted out from under the tablecloth and grabbed one of the man's shoelaces, loosening the knot as he dragged the lace over to the dessert trolley. He quickly tied it around the wheel axle before tying the other end of the lace to the leg of the table they were hiding under.

'NOW THERE'S A BIRD IN HERE!' boomed the woman, pointing at the creature at the waiter's feet. 'A RAVENOUS HAWK IS ATTACKING THE STAFF! IS THIS A RESTAURANT OR A SAFARI?'

The waiter jumped at the sight of Willoughby apparently pecking at his feet and backed sharply away. Unfortunately for him, the dessert trolley and the table followed, surprising the waiter so much he fell backwards, upending the trolley with a crash and sending the table flying. Brandy snaps soared into the air, custard poured over the carpet and profiteroles scattered themselves amongst the astonished diners.

'I HAVE BEEN ASSAULTED BY A RASPBERRY TRIFLE! CALL THE POLICE IMMEDIATELY!'

At her table, Claudia had calmly watched the drama unfold. Her sharp eyes had missed nothing.

'I think,' she said, dabbing her mouth with her napkin as a meringue rolled past, 'I shall skip dessert. I wouldn't want to keep little Gobkin waiting ...'

19

Brother Trouble

Gafferty and Willoughby stopped for breath behind a pile of luggage. As soon as the table started to topple, they had jumped clear and run for the lobby.

'That was brilliant!' Gafferty laughed. 'When you cause distractions, you don't do things by halves. I don't know why people have such a problem with spiders – I love them.'

Willoughby looked pleased.

'I'm glad I did something right, for once,' he said. 'Did you find out the room number?'

'Only just – Room 531.'

'That means it's on the fifth floor. The top floor. And I know a quick way there.'

He led her to the end of a long corridor, where there was a door with the words **FIRE EXIT** on it. Next to it, at ground (or Smidgen) level, there was an electrical socket. Willoughby pulled on the socket's cover, which opened like a porthole. The wiring had been removed – the socket was a Smidgen door into the adjoining room.

'This is the old tower from your atlas,' Willoughby said as they stepped through.

It was not what Gafferty had imagined. Any memory of the tower's ancient history or character was gone. The floor was covered in dull brown carpet tiles. A fire extinguisher hung on the wall. There was nothing else there except a circular metal staircase that wound up to the roof high above like an uncoiled spring. Doors led on to the staircase from each of the hotel's floors. It was clean but empty, its whitewashed walls lit by the hard glare of a fluorescent light.

'I didn't think it would be so … boring,' she said.

'We're not up there yet.'

'Up where?'

'Up *there*.' He pointed to the roof. 'That's home. That's the Roost, of course.'

Willoughby took off his backpack. He pulled out a piece of green cloth and waved it over his head.

'What are you doing?' Gafferty asked.

'Signalling to my brother. You might want to take a step back.'

'Watch out!' a voice called from high overhead. A Smidgen, a teenager, descended into view, hanging from a rope that led all the way up to the ceiling. Like Willoughby, he wore a bird-style crash helmet and jacket.

'There you are, Will!' he said, without noticing Gafferty. He detached himself from the line, which was part of what appeared to be a winching device strapped to his chest, and ran over to Willoughby. 'Look, little bro, I'm sorry I shouted at you earlier. I've checked over your wings, and I reckon a bit of sticky tape here and there and they'll be as right as rain.'

'Are you sure?' said Willoughby, grinning. 'I won't be able to take the exam until they're rebuilt!'

'Never mind about any exam!' said Gafferty impatiently. 'We need to get on with rescuing Gobkin, Willoughby. That woman could be returning to her room at any moment.'

'Woman? Rescue?' said the older boy, as if seeing her for the first time. He frowned. 'Who are you? Who's Gobkin? What's going on, Will?'

'This is Gafferty, Wyn,' Willoughby said uncomfortably. 'I met her at the toy shop. Gafferty, this is my brother, Wynloch.'

'Will, what have you got yourself involved with?' said Wyn, ignoring her. 'You can't go for a minute without getting into trouble. Going to Clabbity's on your own? Bringing outsiders to our home? What are you thinking? And what do you think Uncle Abel and the Elders are going to say? Honestly, Will, you're useless!'

Willoughby looked at his feet, shamefaced. Gafferty pushed past him and stood on her tiptoes to face his brother.

'Listen, Winifred, or whatever your name is,' she said, hotly. 'Your little brother saved my life today – twice! And he's promised to help me rescue *my* brother. He's not useless, he's brave and clever and kind. Now, get out of our way because we've got far more important things to do than worry about what Uncle Abel and his friends are going to say.'

Wyn was taken aback but didn't move.

'It's not allowed,' he said.

'I'm really tired of hearing that,' said Gafferty. 'Come on, Will. We're wasting time.'

'Wyn,' pleaded Willoughby. 'She needs our help. Her

137

little brother's been kidnapped. At least let's hear what Uncle Abel has to say.'

'Fine,' growled Wyn. 'Have it your way.' He reattached himself to the rope and pressed a button on the winch tied to his chest. It automatically began to feed the rope through its cogs, dragging the boy into the air, back up to the ceiling far overhead.

'Don't worry about him,' Will said as Gafferty fumed silently. He produced a similar winch from his rucksack and pulled the straps over his shoulders. 'He's used to me being his baby brother and having to look after me. Our parents are dead, you see. I think the responsibility gets to him sometimes.'

Gafferty bit her lip, guiltily. Wyn was like her: he had been trying to protect Will, just like she was supposed to protect Gob. Only she had failed, badly. Will worried about messing things up, but the truth was Gafferty was far worse. She blinked ashamed tears away.

Unaware, Will clipped his winch to the rope.

'I'm ready,' he said brightly. 'We'll have to piggyback to get you up there.'

Gafferty awkwardly clambered on to his back, glad that he couldn't see her face.

'Oof! You're heavier than I thought,' he said. 'Could

you move that extra spider arm?
It's tickling my ear.'

She glanced up at the
roof: it seemed very distant;
at least five human-sized
floors were between the
ground and the ceiling.

'Ready?' Will called.
He pressed the button on
the winch, and they shot
upwards. The higher they
climbed, the faster the winch
worked until they were zipping
past the doors to each of the
hotel's floors. Gafferty felt a little
sick as they lurched upwards but
was impressed by how fast they
were moving.

'Dad would love one of those
gadgets,' she said. If he ever
spoke to her again, that is.

'The Upliner? We've all got
one. We couldn't live how we
do without it.'

139

They neared the ceiling, which was supported by half a dozen arched beams made from ancient oak. Willoughby pressed another button on the Upliner, and they came to a halt, swinging gently beneath a metal loop that fixed the rope to an arch. He then used the winch to lower them on to the surface of a platform that had been built out from one of the beams. Wyn was waiting for them, looking sullen. He pulled the rope up behind them, then wound it into a coil. Gafferty noticed there was a crate of ropes and loops nearby, waiting to be used by others.

'We're almost there,' Willoughby said. Following Wyn, he guided her to the beam, which had a set of steps carved into it. They led up to a tiny trapdoor in the ceiling.

Gafferty found she was suddenly nervous. Willoughby seemed nice enough. Would the rest of his clan treat her the same way? Or would they take Wyn's view? He had made it clear she was unwelcome. Maybe the Smidgen clans hadn't been friendly to each other. Perhaps they had even been enemies. But there was no turning back now.

Wyn poked his head through the trapdoor then climbed swiftly through it. With an encouraging smile at Gafferty, Will followed.

'OK,' Gafferty said, taking a deep breath. 'Here we go.'

20

The Roost

The first thing Gafferty noticed was the smell of cooking, reminding her of how hungry she was. It was well past supper time and she hadn't eaten anything since middle-meal. It was a good smell, rich and sweet and spicy. The whole roof space was filled with warm, welcoming light. The roof itself rose to a point and on its underside hung loads of boxes. Boxes with windows and doors, connected by rope ladders and platforms, and hung with golden lamps. They were houses! It was a little town crowded into the roof like the nests of house martins, overlooking the floor that formed the tower's attic. The window she had seen from outside gave a view of the setting sun through its stained glass, a sun setting over a world that was a lot bigger than when Gafferty had embarked on her journey to find more Smidgens.

Her curiosity drew her up through the trapdoor and she stepped out on to the huge platform. The floor acted as a large communal space: there was a storage area, what seemed to be a small market, and seating and tables for a sort of tavern. That was where the smell of cooking was coming from. There were more Smidgens than she had ever seen, of all ages and sizes. They were dressed in birdlike clothing, though she could see a few bats amongst them as well. And they were all staring at her or whispering to each other. No one looked pleased to see her.

Willoughby and Wyn were talking to a stern-faced man with a woodpecker-like coat. Will beckoned her over, as a crowd began to form around them.

'You've got some explaining to do, Will,' the man was saying. Will's forehead creased with worry.

'Uncle Abel, I—' he began. Gafferty stepped forward.

'No, *I've* got some explaining to do,' she said. This wasn't time for talking – Gobkin was still in danger and every minute spent pointlessly discussing things was another minute lost.

'You will get your turn to speak, child,' Uncle Abel said curtly. Gafferty ignored him and spoke loud enough

for everyone in the crowd to hear.

'It's not Will's fault that I'm here. It's all mine. I'm Gafferty Sprout. I know I'm an outsider and I might only be a child who's breaking all the rules, but I've got the same needs and dreams as everyone else. I set out to find other Smidgens because as far as I knew my family were the last. All I really wanted was to find some friends.' Gafferty's voice cracked and went quiet. She bit her lip. She thought of Gob, and Mum and Dad, and even horrible little Grub. Everything had gone wrong. 'I didn't mean any harm.'

There was a murmur from the crowd. Not of disapproval but of sympathy. Some of the Smidgens were looking at her kindly. There were good people here, people like Will. *Too small to cause any trouble but big enough to care.* Those were Dad's words. They gave her courage. She took a deep breath.

'And I did find friends – I found Will. He may be my only friend so far but he's also definitely my best friend. Which is just as well, as I need friends more than I ever knew, and I think we all need each other too. My brother has been taken by a witch, or at least a person who is hunting Smidgens. She doesn't care where they're from, whether they're outsiders or not. She's hunting

Smidgens, and a mirror, and she's in this hotel right now.'

There were gasps and mutterings from the Smidgens. Then the crowd parted to let through a small woman, the oldest Smidgen Gafferty had ever seen. She was dressed as an owl, with two large amber jewels in her white hair that resembled eyes. Although she was old, she studied Gafferty keenly.

'A mirror?' the old lady said. 'You're sure, Gafferty Sprout? One of our scouts spotted a woman arriving at the hotel yesterday, not the usual type of visitor. There were strange, unearthly lights emanating from her room today.'

'I told you we had eyes on everything in this town,' Will whispered. 'Lady Strigida knows about magic too. She has visions and things.'

'Yes. A mirror,' said Gafferty to the woman, 'I'm sure that's what she said. The Mirror of Trokarwash or something. I've seen her here, I tell you, and I've seen the horrible, cold mist monster things that she's working with.'

'Trokanis?' The old lady suddenly grabbed Gafferty's hand and dragged her into one of the nearby houses, her grip surprisingly strong. 'Abel, Willoughby – you come along too,' she commanded. Gafferty found herself in a sitting room, lit by a tealight fire. Aside from some sofas made from hotel soap dishes and a table created from a drinks mat from the hotel bar, the room was filled entirely with books and scrolls. The woman urgently began rummaging through them, searching for something.

'What do you know?' said Gafferty. 'And what's it got to do with my brother? Poor Gobkin – we need to help him *now*!'

'Wait,' said Abel, his voice softer than before. 'This could be important. Lady Strigida is the chief of the Elders. She is steeped in the Smidgen-lore. What is it, Strigida? What do you know?'

'A human is pursuing Smidgens,' the old woman said.

'A witch perhaps, or someone with a knowledge of magic, if she keeps the company of ghosts – as I'm sure that's what you saw.'

'Ghosts!' Gafferty gasped.

Strigida found a book, ragged with age, and turned the pages hurriedly. Willoughby nudged Gafferty's arm.

'That was a really good speech out there,' he whispered. 'You impressed them.'

'Thanks. I hope you don't mind me calling you my best friend.'

Willoughby grinned.

'Do I have any choice?' he said. 'The way you argue with your friends makes me sorry for your enemies.'

'Here!' said Lady Strigida. She pointed to a page with a drawing of a diamond shape on it, surrounded by a pattern of strange markings. 'The Mirror of Trokanis. The stories are patchy, forgotten – perhaps forgotten deliberately. For the Mirror, an object of magic, held great power.'

'What did it do?' asked Abel.

'The Smidgens used it for travelling about the town before the Disaster.'

'Like a *kar*?' said Willoughby. 'That sounds a bit of an odd thing to do with a mirror. It doesn't sound magical.'

'If a Smidgen looked into the Mirror,' said Strigida, 'they could travel to another place, as quick as thought. Teleportation, they called it. No need to use the Tangle, you could teleport yourself into a human food store and out again without them ever knowing. It was broken in the Disaster and the pieces scattered.' She threw the book down in frustration. 'It was a time when Smidgens fought each other. So much knowledge was lost in the violence and the years that followed. The three clans ended contact with each other and kept to their homes: the Roost, the Hive and the Burrow.'

'The Hive,' said Gafferty. 'That must be our home! We call it the House, but I always thought it was like a beehive, or an anthill. Except empty, of course. Maybe that's why we always dress as insects and other creepy-crawlies. But that doesn't explain why the woman has taken Gobkin.'

'Who knows the mind of one of the Big Folk? She may have a use for the Mirror if she can put it back together. You don't need to be Smidgen-sized to use it. And to find it, what should she do first? Who is most likely to know the location of the Mirror?'

'A Smidgen!' said Gafferty, her stomach filling with dread. 'She thinks Gobkin might know where it is! But he doesn't ... and when she finds out he doesn't know anything, what will she do with him then?'

Lady Strigida looked at the floor but didn't answer.

21

The Rescue Mission

Giddy with fear, Gafferty ran out of the house. The crowd had mostly scattered. Once the excitement created by the arrival of a stranger in the Roost had passed, people had returned to their business.

'I've got to go!' she called to Willoughby, who was running to keep up. 'I need to – ouch!' She bumped straight into Wyn, who had been waiting outside.

'Move!' she yelled at his face.

He held his hands up.

'Look, I'm sorry for earlier. You were watching out for your brother. I understand. It sounds like you've been through a lot.'

'And it's not over yet,' Gafferty said. 'The longer I

delay, the more likely it is that the witch will be in her room. But … thanks.' She bit her lip. 'I'm sorry I shouted too.'

Abel and Lady Strigida appeared at the doorway. They'd been talking some more.

'We'll send some people with you,' Abel said to Gafferty. 'You can't go on your own. We need to know more about the woman and what she's up to.'

'Thank you,' she said with relief. She could feel tears coming again but she fought them back. 'I've not really thought about how I'm going to rescue Gobkin. I've had some luck so far and I was hoping it would hold. But help is better than luck.'

'We'll get Gobkin home safe and sound,' promised Willoughby.

'Thanks, Will,' she said. And maybe – just maybe – Mum and Dad wouldn't be too angry with her. Though at that moment, she'd rather have faced their anger than anything else in the world, if it meant Gob was with her.

'I'll go with Gafferty,' Wyn said, to her surprise. 'I know my way around the air conditioning system of the hotel. The air conduits are the quickest route to any of the rooms.'

'I'll come too,' said Will.

'No, Will,' said Abel. 'It's too dangerous. But you can't go by yourself, Wyn.'

'The fewer people involved the better,' put in Strigida, gently. 'We don't want this woman working out there are hundreds of Smidgens in the very hotel she's staying in. Leave this to Wyn and Gafferty.'

Will protested, but Abel nodded his agreement.

'We'll be back soon,' Gafferty reassured Will, as Wyn led her to the trapdoor. 'And when this is over, I'll take you on a tour of the Tangle … if that's allowed. There are still loads of adventures to be had.' Will's face brightened slightly but he looked at her sulkily as she waved goodbye and disappeared down the steps.

Wyn strapped a spare Upliner on to Gafferty and showed her the function of each of the buttons. Once she was sure what she was doing, they used their winches to drop them on to the tower staircase at the fifth-floor level. Wyn found and opened a Smidgen-door cut into the wall. The wall was hollow and Gafferty saw a rope ladder inside it hanging down from a metal pipe far above.

'That's the air pipe,' explained Wyn. 'Room 531 is four rooms along. It's not too far at all.'

They clambered up the rope and into the pipe through

a hole sawn into its side. The metal pipe echoed, so they made their way along it as noiselessly as possible, passing over the top of the guests' bedrooms. They could peek at the Big Folk below, snoozing or watching TV, through the vents that kept the rooms supplied with fresh air. *Gobkin would like this*, thought Gafferty, *it's like having a fly's eye view of everything*. Wyn pointed to the next vent.

'That's Room 531,' he whispered to Gafferty.

They surrounded the vent and peered into the room. It was dimly lit by a lamp. The curtains were open, revealing the early evening sky. The room appeared empty.

'She's still not there!' said Gafferty. 'And I can see Gobkin! Look!'

On the table was a small bucket, normally used for holding ice. A tiny figure sat inside it, his arms folded. The sides of the bucket were smooth and far too high for him to climb out.

Wyn took a metal bar from his jacket. Gafferty recognised it as a Big Folk hex key and watched as the teenager used it to prise up the edge of

the vent and prop the metal grid open. There was just enough of a gap for them to squeeze through. Wyn tied a piece of rope around one of the vent slats and fed it through the winch on his chest. Gafferty did the same.

'You go first,' he said. 'I'll follow.'

Gafferty did as directed. She quickly reached the floor and detached herself from the rope. The room was quiet.

'Gobkin!' she yelled, sprinting towards the table. 'Gobkin – it's me! I'm here to rescue you!'

'Gafferty?' Gobkin's voice drifted up from inside the ice bucket.

'I'll have you out of there in a second,' she called.

'No!' Gobkin answered, sounding desperate.

'Don't worry, Gob!' Gafferty was aware she could see her breath as a cloud in front of her. But it only did that when …

'No, Gafferty – they're here! They're waiting for you!'

… when it became colder …

'It's a *trap*!'

The air moved. Gafferty's heart sank. She whirled around as the misty shapes circled her, looking far more solid than she had seen them before. She could hear them laughing, see their faces full of triumph, feel their chill against her skin.

'You stupid ghosts!' she said. 'I know what you are!'

They didn't care and laughed harder, mockingly.

Wyn – where was he? He had been about to follow her! She glanced up at the air duct but there was no sign of him. Had he abandoned her? Had he pretended to be nice, pretended to help her just to get her out of the Roost and away from his brother, leaving her at the mercy of these monstrosities? Gafferty didn't want to believe it. Either way, there was no point him being caught too. Perhaps this was how it should be: Gafferty on her own. Gafferty against the world.

'You can't hurt me, you horrible spooks!' she yelled. 'I'm not afraid of you! Ghosts are just farts with faces!'

Claudia Slymark stepped out of the bathroom, where she'd been waiting.

'You're mistaken, dearest Gafferty!' she said with a smile. 'They can hurt you. You should be very afraid. Very afraid indeed.'

22

The Battle of Room 531

'How fortunate,' said Claudia. 'I appear to have caught a spider. An escapee from the restaurant, perhaps?'

Gafferty groaned.

'You saw me,' she said. 'You knew I was on my way to rescue Gobkin.'

'I merely had to play hide-and-seek until you turned up. I'm glad you weren't too long. These hotel bathrooms are a bit cramped. And Peggy Gums is all elbows.'

One of the ghosts grabbed Gafferty and swept her up on to the table next to the ice bucket.

'I'm sorry, Gafferty,' sobbed Gobkin. 'I tried to tell you!'

'Everything's all right, Gob.' She hoped she sounded brave. 'I'll get you out of there.'

But then what? She glanced around. The table was next to the window, which was open. But they couldn't escape that way – it was on the fifth floor!

'No need,' said Claudia. She walked over to the table and tipped the bucket on to its side. Gobkin rolled out, landing next to Gafferty's feet. 'There – reunited with your brother. Two little Smidgens. *My* two little Smidgens. It's always good to have a spare.'

Gafferty wrapped her arms around her brother and gave him the biggest hug she could.

'I'm so sorry, Gob,' she said. 'This is all my fault. I should never have brought you to the toy shop. Then this witch would never have caught you.'

'It's all right,' he said. 'I'm OK. But she's not a witch, she's just an ordinary thief who knows a bit of magic. Erm … you can stop hugging me now.'

'Very touching,' said Claudia. 'But I've wasted enough time.' Her voice changed, became harsher. 'The Mirror of Trokanis. The Smidgens know where it is. It was broken and the pieces are missing. You will tell me where to find them.'

'I've told this Claudia Slymark person I don't know anything,' said Gob. 'I've never heard of it and I'm sure no such thing exists.'

'Oh no,' said Gafferty, thinking quickly. 'You're wrong. It definitely exists.' *Because if the Mirror doesn't exist*, she thought, *then Claudia Slymark has no reason to keep us alive. We need to play for time.*

'I knew I wasn't being told everything!' said Gobkin, indignantly. 'I'm fed up with this. I want to go home.'

'And you will, Gob.' Gafferty turned to Claudia, whose eyes glittered greedily. 'In fact, why don't we do a deal? I will tell you where the pieces of the Mirror of Trokanis are if you let my brother go.'

Claudia was silent. The ghosts appeared to hold their breath, even though they didn't have any breath to hold.

'No,' snarled the woman, finally. 'There will be no deals. If you don't tell me, then perhaps your parents will. My seekers here will hunt them down. And I'm sure there are other Smidgens in this town. I found you quickly enough and it won't take me long to find them. So why don't you save everyone the pain and tell me what you know.'

'You'll never find the pieces, you horrible thief!' Gafferty shouted defiantly. 'And you'll have to keep on using your spooky friends to do your dirty work because you'll never be teleporting anywhere—'

'Quiet!' spat Claudia. The ghosts stirred uneasily.

What did the child mean? Claudia didn't give them time to think. 'Hinchsniff!' she commanded. 'Gobkin looks pale. I believe he needs to get some air.'

Eager for action, the ghost grabbed Gobkin and carried him to the window.

'Does the little fly want to learn how to fly?' Hinchsniff sniggered. He dangled the boy by his foot out over the street, far below. Gobkin screamed.

'Bring him back!' begged Gafferty, running after them helplessly. 'Please, bring him back!'

'Ah, fresh evening breezes!' Totherbligh teased. 'Very good for the old constitution, you know. Not so much if Hinchsniff drops him, of course. And he can be very clumsy.'

'Smidgen-pancake!' giggled Peggy Gums. 'Nice and flat, dribbled with strawberry jam.'

The old lady ghost bared her fangs at Gafferty, her huge cold form surrounding the tiny girl like a cloud. Gafferty found herself lost inside a thick, eddying, freezing fog, blinded by its swirling shapes, suffocated by its stench of death. She shivered violently and could feel her fingers going numb – she had to fight it, cut through it somehow!

The knife. Her weird glass knife! It didn't like ghosts,

that much she knew! She felt for her scavenger bag as best as she could, slowly reaching inside it. There, a shape she recognised. As she touched it, her hand instantly warmed. She grasped the blade and pulled it free.

The knife lit up like a firework, dazzling white at its centre with a halo of pinkish light that sparked and crackled. Gafferty slashed the ghostly body around her. The knife sent out blasts of rose-coloured lightning, slicing through the fog, as Peggy Gums shrieked with horror and pain. Then with a noise like a kettle boiling uncontrollably her body was ripped apart by great bursts of vapour, knocking Gafferty to her feet and sending her flying across the table. Wisps of the ghost whirled in all directions before disintegrating into nothing.

'What have you done?' Claudia demanded, as Totherbligh cowered at her shoulder. The woman looked wild and furious.

Gafferty tried to pull herself together.

'So much for your spooks,' she said, attempting to sound braver than she felt. 'One down and two to go!'

'She has power, Miss Slymark!' said Totherbligh, fearfully. 'She attacked me with it at the toy shop.'

Claudia saw the knife and her eyes widened.

'It's the Mirror,' she said. 'She has a piece of the Mirror of Trokanis in her hand! *A crystal … the colour of the dawn sky, filled with life force.* Its magical life energy must be reacting against the death energy of ghosts. And she had it all along!'

She advanced towards the table warily. Gafferty picked herself up and ran across to the upturned ice bucket. She gave it a shove and the object rolled on its curved side along the table to the edge by the window. Instead of falling to the floor, it wedged itself in the narrow gap between the table and the wall. Gafferty bounded over it, using it as a bridge to get to the window.

'I'm on my way, Gob!' she called. Hinchsniff, floating outside the window, eyed her with a mixture of fear and hate as he clung on to Gobkin. The little Smidgen whimpered miserably.

'You're not going anywhere!' cried Claudia.

'Be careful, Miss Slymark,' pleaded Totherbligh. 'She has the power to destroy ghosts!'

'She might have power,' said Claudia, 'but I am *not* a ghost. And now she must deal with me.'

23

Night Flight

Gafferty's answer was to scramble out on to the window sill, a narrow stone ledge that ran the length of the hotel. She tried not to look at the ground so far below. Perhaps she could climb down the side of the building? She still had her pin hooks and fishing line, as well as the Upliner. But what about Gobkin? She glared at Hinchsniff and waved the knife at him. It still glowed but there was no more lightning – he must be out of reach of its power.

'Keep that thing away!' he growled. 'I'm holding on to your little brother. If anything happens to me, he gets it!'

'Gafferty!' wailed Gobkin.

'Give me the knife,' commanded Claudia from inside the room.

Gafferty was flummoxed. There was nothing she could do. Claudia charged towards the window, her wiry arms easily dragging the table out of her way. She didn't look like the kind of person who was going to let a five-storey drop bother her.

In the corner of her eye Gafferty saw a shape moving through the darkening sky, turning and banking above them. Then like a bird it swooped down and flew straight through the ghost's body, spearing it like a dart. Small hands reached out for Gobkin and tore him from the phantom's grasp, carrying him away over the rooftops. Hinchsniff was as surprised by the sight as Gafferty. Claudia reached the window.

'What was that?' she roared.

Before anyone had time to react, another bird shape sailed into view, though it flew slower and wobblier. As it neared, Gafferty could see it wasn't a bird – it was Will, hanging on to a glider! He landed on the ledge with an inelegant bump, his wings folding together. They were just out of Claudia's reach but Hinchsniff lunged at them. Gafferty brandished the knife at him and he retreated with a scowl. Claudia began to pull herself through the window, her fearless cat-burglar instincts taking over.

'Gafferty!' Will said. 'No time to explain! Wyn's got Gobkin.' He threw her a looped and padded piece of rope with a clip on one end that was fastened to the glider. 'Now put this harness around you and hang on.'

Gafferty put the knife in her belt and did as she was told. The glider was a triangle of fabric, perhaps a hotel pillowcase, with a frame made of wood and coat hanger wire. Gafferty could see how they might be used for gliding, like a cross between a human hang glider and a kite.

'Now, on three, we go. One ... two ... three ... GO!'

Gafferty had never been so terrified and yet so excited. They jumped straight into the sky, Claudia's outstretched hand grabbing at their heels. Gafferty tried to scream as they plunged downwards but her mouth filled with air. Then the breeze caught them, and the unfolded wings took them soaring upwards, circling over the roof of the hotel. Claudia was left behind, glaring up at them furiously.

Gafferty glanced at Will, who beamed at her. He obviously felt at home in the air.

'So, you do have wings!' she said.

'They're Wyn's spare set.'

'And they actually fly.'

'What did you think they were for? Decoration?'

'Well, I have spider legs, but I don't spin webs out of my bum.'

'You should do something about that.' Willoughby grinned. 'Could be useful in these situations. Look, there's Wyn up ahead. He's managed to clip your brother in so he's safe.'

'I thought Wyn had abandoned me,' said Gafferty.

'No! He wouldn't do that, but he's level-headed too. He doesn't dive into trouble without thinking.'

'Like me, you mean.'

'Exactly. He came running back for help after you were caught by the woman and we launched our gliders straight away. His plan is to head far from the Roost, so she doesn't guess where we live.'

Gafferty peered behind her, back to the hotel. She could see Claudia's silhouette against the window. What was she doing?

'She's … she's climbing on to the ledge,' Gafferty said.

'What's she thinking? She's on the fifth floor!'

Claudia launched herself into the air. Gafferty took a sharp intake of breath but the woman didn't fall. She was floating. The two remaining ghosts were carrying her high above the ground, on a cushion of phantom fog.

'She's flying! Will – she's flying after us!'

Will looked back. He whistled like a bird, a signal to Wyn. The other glider performed a sharp turn and flew back so the two gliders were side by side. Gobkin waved at his sister.

'Wait till Mum and Dad hear about this!' he yelled across.

Gafferty put the thought out of her mind. She could imagine Dad's face all too well.

'Claudia's chasing us!' she yelled, pointing back at the cloud following them. Wyn nodded.

'We'll split up,' he said. 'I'll take Gobkin over the town and if they follow, we can lose them in the alleys.'

He leaned into his glider and it banked away. Will steered the other glider in the opposite direction. Claudia's ghost cloud pursued them without hesitating. Gob was safe for now.

'It's the knife,' said Gafferty. 'She wants it. We can't let her have it!'

'We'll keep flying,' said Will. 'We're safe as long as we can keep ahead and away from the Roost.'

'That could be a problem,' said Gafferty.

Claudia and her seekers were shadowing them relentlessly. She didn't seem to be in any hurry, floating gracefully through the darkening sky, and yet they were rapidly catching up with the little glider, like an approaching thunderstorm.

'What's she got in her hand?' said Gafferty. 'Will, she's got a gun! She's firing—!'

'Jumping jackdaws!' said Will, just as they heard a popping sound from the ghost cloud. 'She's fired a grappling hook! She's trying to bring us down.'

A huge metal anchor on the end of a rope sailed through the air towards them. Hauling on the controls, Will banked the glider steeply, turning the craft back in the direction of the hotel. It dodged the anchor by a hair's breadth, narrowly avoiding having a hole punched straight through it. But the rope clipped the tip of one of the wings as it sailed past and

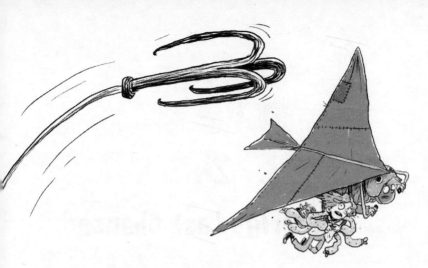

sent the craft spinning around.

'I can't control it!' Will yelled as Gafferty clung on for dear life.

The glider hurtled towards the hotel. Will battled to keep the flying craft's nose up, to soften the landing as best as he could. They bounced off a chimney pot and smashed into the roof tiles, a loose slate ripping the glider's wing fabric and snapping its supports, sending them skittering down the steep slope of the roof. Gafferty screamed: dragged by the wreckage of the glider, they were heading straight for the edge of the building. There was nothing between them and the terrifying drop to the ground below.

24

Gafferty's Last Chance

They were flung over the gutter into the empty night air. In the split second in which she dared to open her eyes, Gafferty saw trees and shrubs and concrete far beneath her. *Please let us land in the trees*, she thought as they plummeted earthwards. *At least then we might survive this awful mess I've caused.*

At that moment Gafferty's harness pulled back against her chest with such force that she would have cried out, had she been able to breathe. She risked a peek, glancing quickly around her. The glider had come to a sudden stop, its torn wing snagged on the hotel's guttering. They were literally hanging by threads, slung beneath the remains of the glider like a pair of puppets, saved only by their harnesses.

Don't look down, she thought. *Don't. Look. Down.*

Beside her, Will moaned something she couldn't understand. He appeared unhurt, just stunned.

'Don't worry, Will,' she said softly, though she wasn't sure he could hear. 'I'm going to get us out of this.'

Rule Four – we meet again, my old friend, she thought. Gafferty's Upliner had smashed in the crash, though it had probably saved her from breaking some bones. Will still had his undamaged Upliner fastened to his chest, and a coil of rope attached to his hip. Perhaps if she could fix one of her pin hooks to the rope and throw it on to the roof, she could use the Upliner to drag them to safety. Then they would have to wait for the Roost Smidgens to come and rescue them. She leaned over to grab the rope. There was a sickening tearing sound from above her. The glider was slipping. If she moved again, she could unbalance them completely.

'We're trapped!' she said. 'What now?'

When she saw the little glider crash-land, Claudia urged her ghosts to carry her back to the hotel.

'Let us grab them for you, Miss Slymark,' implored Hinchsniff as they neared the building.

'No,' said Claudia coldly. She'd had enough of ghosts and magic for one day. The supernatural couldn't be trusted: it was time she went back to doing what she knew best.

Her grappling hook was lost so she launched herself from the cloud, even though they were high above the ground, and landed neatly against the hotel's wall. She gripped the stonework with her fingertips and toes, her highly trained muscles easily supporting her body weight. This was where she belonged. She was a cat burglar at heart, nimbly scaling a building in search of valuables. The damaged glider was a short climb away, and then this sorry episode would be over. Gafferty Sprout would learn just how angry Claudia could be. She now had a spare bottle hanging around her neck. With a bit of squishing, Gafferty might well fit inside it – if she was lucky.

Gafferty reached for the Upliner once more. Slowly this time, trying to keep the glider steady. Will stirred.

'Gafferty … ?' he mumbled.

'Will, keep still! Are you OK?'

'I'm all right, I think. What's happened?' He tried to turn. The glider shuddered ominously.

'Don't move!' Gafferty tried to sound calm but had a

suspicion she was practically screeching. 'Whatever you do, don't move. We're hanging from the guttering of the hotel. But only just! We've got to get out of here – fast!'

'What can we do?' Will looked panicked. 'If only I was a better pilot. This is the second set of wings I've broken in as many days! I'm going to be in so much trouble!'

'Not if we plunge to our deaths first! Keep still, Will. None of this is your fault. It really isn't. Give me one end of your rope – slowly – and I'll throw a line up on to the roof. It'll be exactly like when we hitched a ride on that Big Folk umbrella.'

Will nodded and gently passed the rope to her. As he carefully threaded the other end into the Upliner, he glanced up suddenly.

'Gafferty, there's another glider coming towards us,' he said, peering into the dark. 'It's Wyn!'

'He shouldn't have brought Gobkin back here,' Gafferty said, trying to follow his gaze. 'It's too dangerous.'

'I don't think that's Gobkin he's with.'

The glider was flying unsteadily, as if it were carrying a heavy cargo. Alongside the teenager, another figure was hanging from the wings, someone who looked extremely uncomfortable. There was no mistaking the beetle leather coat.

'That can't be ...' said Gafferty, both thrilled and horrified at the same time. 'It's not ... it's not Dad, is it? He's shouting something – what's he saying?'

'He says "You're grounded", and some other words which aren't very polite.'

'That's definitely Dad!' Gafferty waved frantically, then immediately wished she hadn't. The glider lurched, the tear now a nasty scar across the fabric of the wing. If they didn't do something soon, it wouldn't be long before the wing gave way completely.

Wyn was also shouting at them, pointing to the wall below. Gafferty looked down and felt her stomach turn over.

She couldn't decide which was more terrifying: the sight of the drop, or the sight of Claudia Slymark climbing swiftly towards them.

As gently as she could, she hunted in her scavenger bag for a hook. She took the crooked pin and pushed it through the fibres of the rope until it was fastened in place. Frost began to form on the metal. Gafferty recognised the signs instantly.

'Miss Slymark has forbidden us from helping,' said the ghost that filled the air around Gafferty. 'She must be in an awfully bad mood. It doesn't bode well for you, I'm afraid.'

'A shame she wants to spoil our fun,' snarled the second ghost, its sinewy arms shoving the bulk of the first one aside. 'Maybe she'll let us play with the little birdie.'

'Gafferty!' There was a roar from the wall below. Claudia was close. 'Give me the knife, girl!'

'Go away,' shouted Gafferty, looking about for a place where the hook might catch.

The first ghost lowered itself near her face. She could feel her hair freezing.

'Was it true, what you said, about the Mirror?' it whispered. 'That if she had it, she wouldn't need us any more?'

'Why don't you go and ask her?' snapped Gafferty. 'But

177

think: if my knife can hurt you so much, what will *all* the pieces of the Mirror do?'

The ghost shivered. The glider shifted again.

'Throw the rope!' cried Willoughby. 'Hurry!'

From above, a tiny bundle plummeted past them, trailing smoke, dropping through the vaporous bodies of the two ghosts. The effect on them was immediate. They recoiled from the bluish haze, choking and spluttering, as if it were poisonous, although it smelt sweet to Gafferty, like flowers.

'The Roost are in flight!' cried Will, pointing to the sky. Gafferty looked up and could just make out a glider far above them in the darkness. Then another glider appeared, and another, and another, until there was a whole flock of little Smidgen birds circling the hotel. Each glider's pilot was throwing the little smoking bundles, which left a fragrant, blue fog in the air. The ghosts were forced to retreat, wheezing horribly.

It didn't work on Claudia, however. A few of the gliders, including the one carrying Wyn and Dad, buzzed close to her as she climbed, attempting to distract her, but Claudia resolutely carried on, swatting at the little aircraft as if they were flies.

'This is your last chance, Gafferty,' the woman called,

breathing heavily as she heaved herself up, handhold after handhold. 'Give me the knife. Or will I have to pick it out from what's left of your body after it hits the ground?'

It *was* Gafferty's last chance. She flung the rope as hard as she could over her head. The hook hit the gutter. She pulled on the line, to check it was secure. It was! And in the nick of time. With an awful shredding noise, the glider began to slide steadily downwards. In a moment there would be no more material left to tear. Gafferty threw her arms around Will's shoulders, wriggling out of her harness so that she dangled precariously from his back. If she let go of him now it would be the end of her.

'Unclip your harness,' she yelled in his ear, as the glider began to drop. 'And take us out of here!'

Will did as he was told, the harness releasing him just as the broken glider finally fell from the gutter. It tumbled to the ground, so far beneath them the wings appeared as only a small white scrap of cloth. The two of them hung from the rope Gafferty had thrown, swinging dangerously from side to side. Will fumbled for the button on his Upliner.

'Where is it?' he muttered.

'Will! Quickly!' Gafferty shrieked. It was too late. There was Claudia's hand, looming up and grasping for them, the woman's face a mixture of anger and satisfaction.

'Give in, Gafferty,' she growled.

'No! Press the button, Will! Do it NOW!'

Will's fingers found the button and he hit it with a purposeful thump. The Upliner whirred into life and they soared upwards, the jolt almost shaking Gafferty off from Will's back. But it wasn't quick enough: Claudia's reach was too long, her movements too fast. She clawed the air in front of them and … was still. As the two Smidgens flew to safety, the woman's hand froze, ice coating her fingers, her skin turning blue. Claudia was as unmoving as a statue, her frosted face permanently fixed in an expression of surprise. She fell away from the wall of the hotel, her limbs stuck in position as if she were climbing an invisible mountain. She toppled backwards and down, and Gafferty was unable to take her eyes off the horrible sight. At the last second, a ghostly cloud rushed to surround the woman, catching her safely in a blanket of mist just before she hit the ground. One of the ghosts looked back up at the Smidgens and, even though it was difficult to tell from that height and in the darkness, Gafferty was sure that it smiled at her.

25

Next Steps

It was Dad who pulled her away from the edge of the building, hugging her tightly to his chest as he carried her up the slope of the roof and out of danger. Gafferty thought he might be crying but it was too dark to see his face. Wyn fetched his brother and together they made their way back to the Roost on foot via a secret door in the chimney, Gafferty still in her father's arms. Exhausted by the events of the day and lulled by Dad's careful steps and the warmth of his body, she nodded off into a deep, dreamless sleep.

She awoke in her own bed. For a moment she was confused. She had to get up. There were things to do. Today was when she normally hunted in the factory, wasn't it? Then she remembered.

She sprang out of bed and ran to the kitchen. Mum, Dad, Gobkin and Grub were all sat at the table, as if nothing had happened, busily eating breakfast. Gafferty's tummy rumbled – she'd not eaten anything since midday the day before. Gobkin grinned at her, like he did when he knew she was in trouble for something.

'Did I imagine yesterday?' she said. 'And more importantly, why didn't you wake me for breakfast?'

'It's not you that should be asking questions, young lady,' growled Dad, getting to his feet, 'after the run around you've given us! Now, get dressed! Mum will bring you some food. I need to tidy up as, thanks to you, we're expecting visitors.'

Visitors! Something that had never happened at the House, at least not in her lifetime. It was like her wishes were coming true. She dashed back to her bedroom, dragging on her clothes. Mum brought Gafferty a fried bean sandwich, stroking her daughter's untidy hair while she ate, sitting on the bed.

'We thought we'd let you sleep in after everything you'd been through,' Mum said. 'We had such a fright when Gobkin appeared with the Smidgen-lad and told us what had happened. Gafferty Sprout, as I live and breathe,

I could take all the worries you've given us these past couple of days and make a whole quilt of care!'

Dad appeared at the door.

'I'm sorry, Mum, Dad,' Gafferty said. 'I really am. I've been so stupid. And Gobkin – is he OK?'

'He's never better,' said Dad, his voice warmer than before. 'He was as ravenous as a termite when he came back but that's all. And he's taken a shine to that Wynloch fellow. Smidgens flying! I've never heard the like. And *me* flying too! First and last time, as well. My guts didn't take to it, that's all I'm going to say.'

'You know what happened?' said Gafferty. 'You know about the Roost … and Claudia Slymark and the Mirror and everything?'

'Young Wibbly Wobbly, or whatever his name is, he told us the parts Gob couldn't.'

'Willoughby!' said Gafferty. That meant he was all right too.

'He seems like a nice boy,' put in Mum.

'We were going out of our minds, wondering where you were,' Dad said. 'Then to hear that my daughter, my firstborn, that I brought into the world with my own hands, as your mother lay there exhausted from labouring for hours, whose tiny naked body I held in my arms—'

'Dad! You're being embarrassing.'

'My daughter … being stalked by ghosts and burglars! We could hardly believe it!'

'I put up a fight, Dad. You'd be proud.'

'And I am. We both are. You don't have anything to prove to us. You only have to talk to us, especially if you're wanting to have daft ideas.'

Gafferty nodded, gratefully.

There was a knock at the door. Lady Strigida appeared, along with a shy Will. He had the same worried face as when she had first met him. Gafferty put down her half-finished sandwich and held out a greasy hand to him. He took it and gave it a squeeze.

'Thanks for rescuing me again,' she said. 'That was a fancy bit of flying.' His worried look disappeared, replaced by a smile.

'That's what best friends do,' he replied. 'The whole of the Roost is talking about it, especially after so many gliders came to help. Their smoke trails were made from burning lavender. It's a ghost deterrent, according to Lady Strigida.'

The woman smiled.

'I've news,' she said. 'Claudia Slymark is gone, or at least she has checked out of the hotel. No one saw her leave, but Room 531 is empty.'

'Is she gone for good?' asked Gafferty. 'I bet she's mad at her ghosts for putting the freeze on her. They seemed very worried about her finding the Mirror.'

'Perhaps she has gone for good, and perhaps not. Clearly, she is determined. She may still be seeking the Mirror of Trokanis, now that she knows at least one piece of it exists.'

'The knife!'

'It's under your pillow,' said Mum, reading her thoughts. 'It's safest with you, at least for now.'

'The question is, who is employing Claudia to seek the Mirror in the first place?' continued Strigida. She sat down on the bed beside Gafferty, her old eyes wrinkled with concern. 'We need to think about what to do next. Two of the clans have been reunited, and the Mirror is making itself known, emerging from the dust of the past. Why? Maybe there is something larger at work. Maybe it is time for the three clans to come together after all these years.'

Gafferty lay back on the bed. Up above her, in its corner of the bed nook, the little spider sat silently. The spider that had found the page in the atlas showing the Smidgenmoot, that had sent her on this adventure.

'I want to help,' she said. 'I think it's something I'm meant to do. There's a whole big wide world out there that I never knew existed. I want to explore it.'

'All in good time,' said Mum firmly. 'Enough adventures for now. I just want to enjoy having my daughter back in her home. I've heard quite enough about ghosts, magic and mirrors for a while.'

'But, Mum ...'

'Aye, there's plenty of time,' added Dad, taking the other half of her sandwich and stuffing it into Gafferty's open mouth. 'Because, dearest daughter, after all you've been up to behind our backs you are absolutely, completely, positively, flipping well GROUNDED.'

Acknowledgements

This is a big story about little people and, like all books, it needed a big cast of big people to make it happen. Firstly, I'd like to thank my editor Lucy Mackay-Sim, whose questions, creativity and patience helped to make sense of the bucketload of ideas sloshing around in my head. Secondly, thank you so much to illustrator Seb Burnett, who brought the world of the Smidgens spectacularly to life under a tricky set of circumstances, and basically saved everyone's bacon. Thirdly, thank you to everyone at Bloomsbury – designers, copy editors, Marketing and Sales – who helped to get the book out into the world and in front of readers. Finally, to the bloggers, librarians, booksellers, teachers and lovely readers who say nice things and make it all worthwhile – THANK YOU!

Look out for
more adventures with

The SMIDGENS

COMING SOON!

When Archie McBudge inherits a
HAUNTED chocolate factory,
he's bitten off more than he can chew!

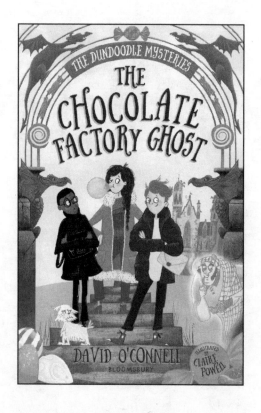

Read on for a sneak peek!

AVAILABLE NOW

1

Archie stared up at the portrait of the old man. It had winked at him, hadn't it? He was sure of it. No, he must be imagining things. This spooky old house was playing tricks with his mind.

He was sitting in the very grand library of the very grand Honeystone Hall, surrounded by books – how could anyone own so *many* books? – and ancient, rickety and *very* dusty furniture. Were all the cobwebs real or were they specially delivered by the We'll-Make-Your-Home-Look-Creepy Company? Mum sat in the chair next to him, fidgeting like she had spiders dancing in her underwear and too preoccupied to pay any attention to misbehaving artwork. Had the portrait winked at him again? It hadn't. Had it? It HAD! It even grinned a little. This place was seriously WEIRD.

He dragged his eyes away from the painting which hung above the very grand fireplace.

'What are we *doing* here?' he whispered for the hundredth time.

'I don't *know*,' Mum whispered back. She gave the sparrow-like man shuffling papers, who sat in front of them, a sharp look.

'Can we get on with … *things*, Mr Tatters?' she said. 'We've come all the way from Invertinkle.'

'Of course, of course, dear lady,' said the lawyer amiably. 'Some of the details of this … *situation* are unusual. I was just checking a few particulars, but now we can proceed.' He cleared his throat dramatically.

'Archie McBudge,' said Mr Tatters, peering at the boy through a pair of grubby spectacles. 'You are a very fortunate young man. Very fortunate *indeed*. Great things lie in store for you.'

Archie had never thought he was destined for Great Things. A few Medium-Sized Things perhaps. 'Medium-sized' always sounded manageable. Great Things sounded like a *lot* of responsibility and he wasn't the ambitious type.

'Really?' was all he could say. *What was going on?*

'Whilst we mourn the recent *tragic* loss of your

great-uncle, Archibald McBudge ...' said Mr Tatters, pointing a bony finger towards the painting – *the* painting! He had a *Great-Uncle Archibald?* '... owner of McBudge's Fudge and Confectionery Company, and a dear, personal friend of mine ...' Archie's jaw dropped. McBudge's Fudge! He'd never even known Great-Uncle Archibald existed, but everyone knew McBudge's Fudge. It was the softest, sweetest-tasting, melt-in-the-mouthiest, fudgiest fudge you could buy. The best in the world. Archie had always been pleased he shared his name with a company that made something so famously tasty, but he'd never thought there might be an actual family connection! And from the look on Mum's face, she hadn't either. She started to say something but was interrupted by Mr Tatters giving his beaky nose a good blow.

'Whilst we mourn his loss,' the lawyer repeated, dabbing his eyes, 'I am very pleased to tell you that your great-uncle remembered you in his will.' He picked up a leather-bound folder. Archie and Mum looked nervously at each other. Nobody had ever left them anything in a will before. They'd never known anyone with any money! All they knew was that Mr Tatters had sent them a letter asking them to drive all the way to the little town of Dundoodle, tucked between a mountain and a

'And Honeystone Hall?' said Archie, looking around him. 'Can we come and live here? There must be over a hundred rooms in this place!' And a very odd painting, though he didn't mention that.

'*And* Honeystone Hall,' said Mr Tatters. He snapped the folder shut. 'Fudge fortune. Fudge factory. Fudge shops. Fudge … urm, *Honey*stone Hall. The whole lot. Even the gardening tools.'

I must have put my lucky underpants on today, thought Archie. He looked up at the portrait of Great-Uncle Archibald. The old man in the painting winked at him again. And this time, Archie winked back.

2

'There's one more thing,' said Mr Tatters, reaching into his jacket pocket. 'Your great-uncle left you this letter.' He handed Archie a crumpled envelope. A surprisingly steady hand (Great-Uncle Archibald looked *ancient* in the portrait) had written on it in thick caramel-brown ink:

To the heir of the Chief of the Clan McBudge.

'The heir,' said Mr Tatters, catching Archie's puzzled look. 'That would be you. Old Mr McBudge intended for you to read this in private. Why don't you go and explore whilst your mother and I discuss the legal paperwork and whatnot? I'm sure you'll find plenty of quiet spots in the house to read.'

He was being dismissed. The grown-ups had grown-up things to talk about. With a nod from Mum, Archie ran out of the library, clutching the mysterious letter. His head was spinning. He was … he was *rich*! And Honeystone Hall belonged to *him*. Him and nobody else. Except maybe the ghost of his great-uncle. What had been going on with that painting? He pushed it out of his mind. There were plenty of other things to think about. Great Things. It would take him a week just to explore the house, never mind the gardens and the factory.

Archie wandered along a passageway, pondering which of the doors to try first. Everything – furniture, pictures, wallpaper – looked *very* old and was covered in a ghostly layer of dust. The stillness was deathly. *Plenty of quiet spots*, Mr Tatters had said. Spots? This was practically measles.

He tried one door. It was a cupboard, filled with moth-speckled coats. Another door revealed an old-fashioned laundry room, with sinks and mangles and drying rails. So far, so disappointing. Yet there was something else. In each room Archie could feel a presence, like someone – some*thing* – had left just moments before. He shivered.

Finally, he chose a large green door with a dark metal handle. With a satisfying clunk, it opened and light poured into the shadowy passage. He took a step backwards as he was struck by the heat and smell of earth. Ferns, palm trees, vines and orchids lay before him, bathed in a balmy mist and occupied with the business of growing and flowering and generally being alive and leafy. Had he stumbled into a different world? Transported to a desert island? He half expected a dinosaur to lumber into view.

'It's a giant greenhouse,' he said aloud. The glass roof was as high as the Hall itself. The warmth, light and life were a marked contrast to the rest of the house and the dreary wintry world outside it. But it had the same watchfulness about it. Something hidden had its eye on him.

Archie followed a path amongst the plants and perched on a twisted tree root that had pushed its way up through the tiled floor. He opened the envelope and pulled out a crisp piece of paper covered with the same caramel-coloured writing.

Dear Archie (the letter began),

Mr Tatters must have told you by now that you are my heir as Chief of the Clan McBudge, as well as heir to the McBudge Fudge fortune. I have no doubt this will have come as a surprise to you. Knowing you would inherit one

day, but wanting you to have a normal life for as long as possible, your father kept his family connections a secret.

So Dad knew all along! Archie smiled. Dad loved secrets. He wished Dad was here now.

Your father was a clever man. Having lots of money can do strange things to people. And the desire for money can make people go bad. Very bad. You must always remember this!

But who better to run a chocolate factory than a child? Children understand fudge and sweets and chocolate far better than grown-ups. However, it is a great responsibility.

You must prove you are worthy of your inheritance, worthy of the name McBudge! So I have set you a test, in the form of a treasure hunt, to see just how canny you are ...

There are six items you must collect, and six clues to find them. Once you have them all, a greater seventh treasure awaits you! But keep it secret! Others will go to any length to get it first!

Others? What did that mean?

The first clue will appear very soon. Keep your eyes open and your taste buds ready! You may find help in the strangest ways. Dundoodle is an odd place – expect the unexpected ...

Good luck!
Your great-uncle, Archibald McBudge.

Archie realised he was holding his breath. His heart was beating fast. A test? A treasure hunt?

P.S. Look behind you.

'If you ask me,' said a voice just by his ear, 'you're in a whole lot of trouble, Archie McBudge.'

Have you read all of
THE DUNDOODLE MYSTERIES?

AVAILABLE NOW